Country Music Country

REVIEWS OF *COUNTRY MUSIC COUNTRY*

Bruce Hunter writes with bold restraint and a poet's sensibility. His blue-collar characters walk the tight line of their lives into the common universe that includes us all.

— Wayson Choy, *Saturday Night*

Focusing on a group of working class kids born in 1953, it's terrifically evocative of this city in the 1960's. *Country Music Country* wrestles the theme of the call of the west into an anguished coherence. A book that sounds to me like "authentic Calgary", the real thing.

— Ken McGoogan, *Calgary Herald*

Country Music Country reflects a landscape that is gritty, high-spirited and straight-forwardly blue collar. The 11 stories are clearly the work of a poet: they are precise, detailed and subtle. At times, as characters from one story pop up in another, you forget these are individual stories and think you are reading a novel. Hunter's unflinchingly realistic stories remind us how tough it really is to have life "all figured out".

— Lynne Van Luven, *NeWest Review*

There's a subtlety to this writing . . . A subtle touch that reminded me of *New Yorker* stories — these endings that have slight illuminations — like the unexpected charity of a mother. And in addition to the subtlety, there is a hint of wistfulness about this book, a loss of childhood, neighbourhoods have disappeared over the decades. And the closest parallel I could think of was the early stories of Guy Vanderhaeghe, so you've got poignance, beautiful language and no tripping into sentimentality.

— Antanas Sileika, CBC - *The Arts Tonight*

Country Music Country

Bruce Hunter

Thistledown Press Ltd.

© Bruce Hunter, 1996
Second Printing, August, 1998
All rights reserved

No part of this publication may be reproduced or transmitted in any form or by any means, graphic, electronic or mechanical, including photocopying, recording, or any information storage and retrieval system, without permission in writing from the publisher. Requests for photocopying of any part of this book shall be directed in writing to CanCopy, 6 Adelaide Street East, Suite 900, Toronto, Ontario, M5C 1H6.

Canadian Cataloguing in Publication Data
Hunter, Bruce, 1952–
Country music country

ISBN 1-895449-58-8

I. Title.
PS8565.U578C68 1996   C813'.54   C96-920054-4
PR9199.3.H857C68 1996

Book design by A.M. Forrie
Cover art by Kathi Posliff
Set in 11pt Carmina Lt.
by Thistledown Press

Printed and bound in Canada by
Veilleux Printing
Boucherville, Quebec

Thistledown Press Ltd.
633 Main Street
Saskatoon, Saskatchewan
S7H 0J8

Thistledown Press gratefully acknowledges the financial assistance of the Canada Council for the Arts, the Saskatchewan Arts Board, and the Government of Canada through the Book Publishing Industry Development Program for its publishing program.

For Rosemary

*And for the memory of my grandmothers,
Robina Kean Hunter, who took me fishing, and Lavinia Begg
Hunter who taught me
that to wander sometimes is not a bad thing.*

Acknowledgements

The author is grateful to the editors of the following magazines in which the stories first appeared:
Fiddlehead, "Hard Labour", "Snake Island"; *Dandelion*, "Harker's Dam", "The Many Happy Returns of Kenny Dawes"; *Zymergy*, "Blood Brothers"; *Grain*, "Manitoba Maple", "Country Music Country", "519"; *Canadian Fiction Magazine and Litterae*, "Arthur"; *Canadian Forum*, "Tulip Soup".

"The Many Happy Returns of Kenny Dawes" also appeared in the anthology *Glass Canyons*, published by NeWest Press. "Arthur" will appear in *Reading Writing*, published by Nelson Canada. "Country Music Country" was nominated for the 1995 Western Magazine Awards for excellence in fiction. "Harker's Dam" was a winner in *Dandelion* magazine's national fiction contest in 1995.

Thanks also for their support to: Burke Cullen, Barry Dempster, Helen Carmichael Porter, Irene Kanurkas, Barb Ritchie and Jon Redfern. A special thanks to Seán Virgo for his editorial input.

Contents

BLOOD BROTHERS 9

ARTHUR 23

HARKER'S DAM 39

BAD EYES 57

MANITOBA MAPLE 78

THE MANY HAPPY RETURNS OF KENNY DAWES 96

519 111

TULIP SOUP 125

SNAKE ISLAND 145

HARD LABOUR 157

COUNTRY MUSIC COUNTRY 179

Blood Brothers

"Indian is bad news," he said that day in the old car, "I just want to make money."

Bob Adams' father was a full-blooded Cree and his mother was a blonde-haired Nova Scotian named McNally. Some people said he wasn't a real Indian. Some said he wasn't even a Métis. There you had it. The only real Indian we knew lived in a high-bottomed house out near the slough right in the middle of the landfill where they dumped concrete and asphalt. All we knew was their name was Shot-Both-Legs. We looked in their windows once, but you couldn't see anything because the windows had sheets over them.

Bob Adams wanted to be a white man. Even before the ceremony that day in the old car. Whiter even than the rest of us. Long before we stopped lugging our lunches, tools, six inch spikes and rope borrowed from the shack out behind the church to build our forts in the secret groves along the river.

We all wanted to be Indians. And for a while we thought we were all blood brothers, even Adrian's sister Suzy. Not the Lone Ranger and Tonto kind of stuff. That was dumb we all agreed. The Lone Ranger was candy-ass.

It was Kenny's idea actually, when we were all thirteen. Suzy was twelve but taller than any of us. We had this old Ford sedan, 1948 or '49, we found at the bottom of the cliff on the river road. Windowless, and doorless, bare as a skull, with its roof caved in, stripped of everything but its trunk lid. Once there was an Indian battle on the prairies above that same cliff and before that the Indians had driven buffalo over it.

And it was said that when the river was low, after the spring flood had shorn away the clay bank, you could find the grey teeth of buffalo in the water like pearls among the stones, and that once someone found a ribcage buried in wet spring clay. When he was our age, Al Connacher, the church janitor even found a lever action Winchester just like Chuck Conners used in *The Rifleman*. Its butt was studded with designs made of tacks. He said it was an Indian war rifle. Peter Olenyck's father found a human skull with a bullet hole in it. The man at the Glenbow Museum where they took it said it was from the battle. It was of an Indian boy only sixteen years old who died nearly a hundred years before. Now it sits in a display case in the junior high foyer.

We never found anything. Except survey stakes for the next lap of houses ringing west towards our precious cliff and the river below it. Even as we tore out the stakes with their coloured ribbons, we knew we were and always would be ten or twenty years too late. All of this was lost land. It had been Indian land and now like them, we were losing it too. How many rifles, we wondered, lay buried and then buckled by construction company bulldozers. We wanted a rifle or a skull of our own. It was that strong. We would have given anything to be someone or something else. Like an Indian.

But Bob Adams wasn't one. We wanted him to be. We figured he knew something we didn't. The Indians knew; they just knew things. No matter what we did, he wouldn't. He even got mad at Kenny that day for bugging him about it.

"Real bad news," he'd said bitterly. "I want to make lots of money and get the hell out of here."

That day in the old car he probably didn't even want to be there. But he was. It was the year everything started to come apart on us. Our bodies sprouting out of control. Old friendships turned to fights and we tried one last time to make it right and whole again, looking for whatever had once kept us together.

Each of us brought something. Adrian, a handful of dried sweetgrass. He'd read that this was holy to the Indians. Kenny got the gopher he'd shot with his bow and new razor head arrows. He'd flung its body round and round until it flew, leaving only the gopher tail. Me, I found a rusted paint pail and Bob Adams lent matches for the fire. It was Kenny who suggested we all go in the pail. Inside the old car, the floor had fallen out and the prairie showed through underneath, tatters of cloth hung from the wooden ribs of the roof and it had an animal smell of decaying leather and wood.

Suzy made us stand outside while she went too. Then we added the gopher tail and some sage and we all spit in it for double good luck. We looked up for the sign Adrian promised us. Nothing.

Then we buried the pail full of spit and piss and gopher. We burned the sweetgrass. And waited. Adrian knew more about Manitou than Bob Adams.

We'd all be blood brothers, Adrian said. Bob Adams laughed. The rest of us waited. No rumbles of thunder, no signs. Only the distant crash of rail cars shunted into each other in the yards where the trains were assembled before heading west. The wind blew loudly and insistently as it always did. We waited and listened. But when the five o'clock whistle blew from the high stack over the railyard, we turned back towards town. The next time Bob Adams laughed, Kenny joined in and the rest of us felt tired and a little dumb with our secret.

All Bob Adams wanted to be then was a pool shark but to the rest of us the pool hall was off limits. You had to be sixteen. Bob Adams was taller and darker and had a year on us. He'd lost a grade when they moved down from Rocky Mountain House. And Kenny could fake a confidence none of us had and he flashed his wallet to us later with its tell-tale ring made by the condom he bought in the washroom. Midnight Black he said. There was a whole array of colours from Red Risqué to Passion Purple. And there was a special one called Parisian Delight. Kenny said it was a French letter. The rest of us would have to wait.

Old Willie Harris ran the poolhall upstairs over the car wash which he rented from the Chinaman who owned the building. Willie never made much money from his tables but he also sold hamburgers, french fries and had a series of old fashioned pinball machines. We never understood how he stayed in business because half the time the place was empty.

Willie's pride was a 1906 billiards table he rescued from the billiards parlour downstairs in the old Grain Exchange Building. Most of the time it sat covered with a drop sheet. It cost 25 cents an hour extra to play, but the money wasn't it. This was the pro table. If you were lucky, Willie would let you groom the table with the felt brush and rack the balls for the sharks when they played. To play eight ball or even snooker on a three-quarter size table was one thing, but to stare down the cue for a left bank on a corner pocket across that expanse of brushed green felt! The scrollwork of its pillared base gleamed dark and solid as the bank manager's desk. Willie even had a special light for it. Most times, the pro table sat covered and dark. But by the time the rest of us could even get in the poolhall, Bob Adams was playing that table.

Willie Harris had a silent partner Izzy Meyers who had one good eye and one glass eye that was covered with a patch just like the man in the shirt commercial. Some said he wore the patch to stare people down. Kenny said his real name was Isaac and he was a Jew. None of us admitted then we didn't know what that was, but whatever it was, we wouldn't mind being one either. He was pretty cool, for an adult. By the time we were old enough to pass Izzy Meyers' one good eye, Kenny was a rack boy and Bob Adams had quit school to work at the pipe plant and when school finished in June, Kenny joined him as a driver's helper. The rest of us had only summer jobs. Suzy worked on the desk at the Holiday Inn downtown. Adrian, after working part-time at the library in the new Riverview Shopping Plaza, was sent to the main branch near city hall. I got a job as a helper on the new insurance building downtown.

If Bob Adams was tall and dark in his new black leather blazer, Izzy Meyers was short and white-haired. And he had class to burn. Once Adrian was using the pay phone in the pool hall and asked for some change. Izzy Meyers pulled out a roll with hundred dollar bills on the outside. He gave Adrian a twenty. Kenny explained later that change was high roller talk for small bills. Kenny's father told him that Izzy Meyers was a bookmaker. I'd thought that meant accountant. But Izzy Meyers was also the only one who took us seriously. He invited us to his apartment downtown near the Holiday Inn. All the other adults hung around with each other. Izzy Meyers didn't mind if we hung around his place. The other adults were careful to point out what they had that we didn't. Izzy Meyers didn't bother. But he had four television sets, three telephones and a closet full of suits with matching hats and shoes. We could all watch a different channel at the same time while he talked on the phones in the den and watched the football game. He sure didn't look like much of a sports fan but he watched all the games. One day when he went somewhere with Bob Adams and left us alone for the afternoon, Kenny took us into the bathroom and showed us a container like those you keep dentures in. In it was a glass eye that looked like a half-painted marble.

"It's his spare," he said, "Cause if it isn't, there's just a big black hole under that patch."

Adrian nearly got sick.

Then we went in the kitchen and he got a chair and pulled the screen from the fan above the stove. On top of it were small printed pads of paper.

"Betting slips," he said as he carefully put them back. By the time Izzy Meyers got back we were quietly watching all four channels.

When Adrian's father heard about the betting slips, Adrian and Suzy were forbidden to go there anymore. I was too tired after work to do anything but sleep. But one Friday night there was a tap on my basement window. It was Kenny and Bob Adams. You could smell the sherry over the summer grass.

"Let's go. Down to the river."

"Kenny, be quiet."

My parents' room was upstairs around the corner and my mother slept like a cat, with one eye open and one ear up in case any of us woke.

"Come on, we're going to party. Adams is playing the city-wide next month."

"I gotta work, you guys." I still had four more hours Saturday morning as it was.

"Come on, we're going anyway. Jamtart."

I could hear them rattle the dry sticks of the lilac bushes as they went over the back fence and then my mother's feet on the floor of her bedroom. I pretended to be asleep when she came down the stairs without turning on the lights. Out of the corner of my eye I watched her with her book of devotions clutched in her hand like some kind of spiritual flashlight. But she always knew. She looked out the open window and after a long while said to me, "He is of the race who knows Joseph."

I didn't know what she meant. She liked to tell us those things. It made her seem wiser somehow. Maybe it was just something she heard, or read in one of her inspirational books, but I didn't think she meant Kenny.

When I ran into Adrian one day on the downtown bus coming home we ended up at the Dairy Bar splitting a plate of fries and gravy and guzzling Coke. Me with my hard hat and black tin lunch pail and Adrian already looking spiff in his white shirt with the tie loose and the top button undone, both of us pretending the Coke had rum in it.

"So, you get your marks?" I asked. That was the big question that summer. The grade 12 departmentals.

"It's university. You?"

"Don't know yet. I blew English and math. Passed typing and accounting, can you believe it?"

"How about construction?"

"Secretarial would be more like it. I'm laid off in two weeks."

"There's always the Shops," he said.

I groaned. Both of us knew that was no choice. Like the army with their weird haircuts. The summer before when we were fifteen and none of us had jobs, we met under the bleachers in the park and in the cool shade as our eyes got used to the dark, talked about what we'd do. Sometimes we invented rich girlfriends with blonde hair and names like Suzanne and Kate and who had their own cars.

And that was the summer the city sodded the path down the middle of the park. It was a rut really, worn kitty-corner across the park about six inches deep. Dusty in the summer, mud in the spring and fall, and a frozen path in winter you toed your way home on in a blizzard. When the five o'clock whistle went, you could see the men like Kenny's father leave the railway shops with their steel black lunchpails, bent and grimy as the coalminers we saw on TV. Their feet fell into the rut each morning and night. Like mine, Adrian and Suzy's father worked construction and he drove a brand new Rambler Classic to work, his source of pride. Sometimes when the fog from the river settled on the park, you couldn't see the other end, but always at 5:10 our friends' fathers emerged out this side, guided homeward by their feet. For weeks after the city sodded the park, there was a brilliant green strip watered and tended by a man who came each day with a hose truck. Carefully the men made their way around the new sod, but by the time the leaves dropped from the poplar trees that fall there was a new rut a few feet east of the old.

We all swore on a bottle of mutually swigged Coke we'd never enter either the Shops or the rut. But we watched each other to see who would be first to go and it scared us that this future was so inevitable.

Changing the topic, I said, "You hear about Bob Adams?"

"Yeah, he's favoured in the city-wide snooker match."

"And Kenny just got his "A" license. Lied about his age. He's driving now, even dropped by to show me the rig — and the air horn — my mother sort of went crazy on us. He says he likes working with Adams."

"Oh bullshit. He's lying. If Adams's working for anybody, he's working for Meyers."

"Working?" I hadn't heard any of this.

"Numbers you idiot. He's running numbers. Izzy Meyers has been busted too many times, and the next time he's caught, it's Drumheller, maybe Kingston."

Ever since he'd seen Izzy Meyers' place, Adrian was on this Elliot Ness kick. Adrian's father had one of those old candlestick phones and he'd been practising answering the phone the way Elliot Ness does in *The Untouchables* by snapping the stem up and catching the receiver in midair, but so far he'd only succeeded in nearly giving himself a black eye.

"Where do you get this stuff?" I asked, picking at my fries while our waitress eyed us impatiently.

"Suzy. She sees Adams at the Holiday Inn all the time. He acts like he's on some kind of spy mission or something and besides, Meyers' office is the lounge there. The pay phones."

"I heard Adams moved out of the house but I thought he was making money at the plant. Shit."

"Deep shit. The house dick told Suzy the cops are watching the place."

"Maybe we should warn him."

"He knows. And the cops know too. Part of doing business."

"What about Kenny? He in on this too?"

"He's egging Adams on and he'd be doing it too except Meyers's smart enough to know what a big mouth he has. Might as well go straight to the cops and turn himself in. Besides the dick says that Meyers's got enough money to buy his way out of anything."

Bob Adams placed second in the city-wide later that summer. All of us were there to watch as he leapfrogged the white ball over his opponent's to drop the black into the corner pocket. Rumour had it that Izzy Meyers had money riding on him, but then so did all of us. He was *our* pool shark.

That night after the tournament, we went back to a room Bob Adams rented at the old railway hotel, once a Salvation Army hostel, and now a rooming house. We passed around a victory mug of rye, its acid burning down the back of our throats. The pain of it made us feel good even as we tried not to cough. When Izzy Meyers arrived, he drank none. Instead he smoked intently and when he finished, took the butt from his ivory holder, then pinched another cigarette into it and when the match died, he began to speak using the silence that had fallen as expectantly as the heavy velvet curtains after the preview in a movie theatre and we waited for the feature to begin. We thought he'd talk about the tournament. We were wrong.

"One night in Sinai, between Israel and Egypt in Gaza," he began, looking around the room at each of us in turn as he spoke those words, his one good eye squinting a little as if staring through the lens of a rifle scope, but it was that eye we imagined behind the patch that transfixed us.

"I was a young man as you are now, in the army there. We had gone to town, my friend and I. Drinking much and smoking maryjane, we called it then, and the hashish. When you are young this is not hard to do. Midnight came and my friend said we must go back to our watch. In the army, one does not desert. The army is everywhere.

"So we make our way on the stones as we had before many nights. It did not matter if we see. Our feet were light as our heads. My post is a machine gun in sand bags. Less than two miles away an Egyptian is there too with his gun."

All of us were silent, even the splash of our whisky in the mug seemed loud as the old man stopped to draw on his cigarette, its glowing ash hypnotic as a campfire.

"Me here and there him. Two miles of darkness between us. But soon I start to sleep. The hashish made that easy. So many nights here that no longer am I afraid. Just the terrible boredom. Several times I wake suddenly, like a man at the wheel in a long drive.

"Then there was a sound. Like a foot hitting a stone and then another. Then it stopped. All the fear I'd forgotten, I remember. Then again the sound. I call out for him to identify himself. No answer. It was quiet again. I could see nothing, but I imagine what is there. A tank. Mortars. Egyptian mortars.

"Then more footsteps, this time heavy like a man under a weight. I call out again. No sound. Then after some time, the sound of a foot on stone. I took no chance and I fired. In seconds, there were tracers in the sky and soon the large guns behind me began to fire. Soon the sky began to light with the flares of the Egyptians. And on our line and theirs the searchlights. Later, when the sun came up and the firing stopped, my commander appeared.

"I tell him I'd heard a mortarman. Out in the strip before my gun we found him. With two large baskets tied to his sides, and a dog tied to him. The smell was very bad. Both of them dead, very dead and filled with wounds. A donkey. I had broken the truce between our armies. I left there shortly. There would be no job for me anywhere. And so I lost my eye."

He stopped there, and as he had begun, looked at each of us. He had us and he knew it. What he had said made absolutely no sense. He had the answer but we had to know the question.

It was Kenny who spoke first while the rest of us just sat there.

"You lost your eye. Come off it."

The old man paused. He had been waiting.

"No, exactly, and yes. Cancer. It's the poison we keep inside. Ten years it took for my eye. And then they remove it. But I lost it that night in Gaza."

Bob Adams interrupted them. Looking at Izzy Meyers he said, "You talk like my grandfather."

Even Kenny was quiet. Bob Adams never talked about family.

"His Indian name was Running Buffalo. The name the priest gave him was Adams. The government men came to him. He knew when the rains and snow would come. They used it in their speeches. He was always right."

That was the first time any of us could remember Bob Adams ever admitting to a past of any kind. It would also be the last.

That fall Adrian went to university across town and I went up north to work for the government in the Highways camp. My uncle got me on as a rod man on a road crew and when times were slow I learned to drive graders and Cats. One day a letter came from Adrian with a small clipping from the newspaper. Izzy Meyers was busted and fined $5000 and given two years' probation. He paid the fine and walked.

According to Adrian, who heard from Suzy, one of his regular customers lost five grand on the Grey Cup. The cops didn't want to move in, they liked the old man, but this particular customer was a well-known judge who later was arrested for drunk driving by a greenhorn right out of police college. Bob Adams wasn't caught, but Izzy Meyers gave him enough money to go out to the coast for a while until things cooled off. Sometimes I think Izzy Meyers was the only honest man we knew because he knew the terror that waited in our young hearts.

We never saw Bob Adams again, but when Suzy got married, I came down for the wedding. She and her husband had stayed at a bed and breakfast place in Nanaimo. One day at Horseshoe Bay waiting for the ferry she ran into Bob Adams. He's working for the coast bus lines and married someone named Carol who runs a daycare where they live in White Rock. Kenny works seasonally, meaning between last call and the hair of the dog. He still sees Izzy Meyers sometimes, who runs the casino at the fair grounds and is a fund-raiser for the children's hospital. Apparently his old customers are good contributors. And Bob Adams stays as far away from this town as he can.

Funny how it goes. Guy wants to be a pool shark, his friends want him to be an Indian and he ends up a bus driver.

Arthur

"You'll be all right. Bundle up good." My mother yanked my scarf even tighter bank robber style at the back of my raised hood.

My education, at nine and a half, was not complete in her eyes. Each day contained a verse of inspiration from her worn copy of *One Day at a Time* and some other crucial instruction usually in the form of a story about the weather, people, my dog or whatever else sprang to her mind.

Today it was twenty below zero, not quite Thirty Below, that mystical number where several threes collided in a deadly freeze as she told me once: "At thirty below with a thirty mile per hour wind, exposed flesh freezes in three minutes. That's fifty below by the chill factor." Later, among the piles of magazines under her bed I found the copy of *Readers' Digest*, and there it was, between "Life's Like That" and "Laughter's the Best Medicine" — "Chill Factor — the *Real* Temperature".

"Last year," she said, "a little girl in Altadore had to have a fireman pour boiling water on her tongue because she didn't listen to her mother." She turned and got the grocery money from the counter.

I wondered what this had to do with going out to the store at twenty below. As I stood in the landing in my duffle coat, sucking in all the warm air I could through my scarf, the mittens she'd knitted dangled at my sleeves, with the cord that kept them a pair tugging at the back of my neck and my scarf choking the front. I was embarrassed by that string, but she insisted.

Nine and a half is a cruel age when you start to notice you have idiot strings and others don't. And other kids were only too happy to point it out for you, as they had my old pants with the new elastic waist: "Smarty pants, smarty pants," they'd hollered, the cry ringing in my ears for weeks. I didn't even try to explain what her effort to extend the life of outgrown pants had cost me as she fished them out of the bottom of the closet.

"Never, ever, put your tongue on metal when it's this cold. Not on the fence, anything. The fire department couldn't do a thing and there she stood with her tongue on the aluminum door until they put boiling water on it." It had never occurred to me, until now, to put my tongue, lips or anything else for that matter on the big aluminum door with the curly cues and our family initial proudly hanging in the centre. She gave me the grocery note for Mr. Waterfield which I tucked into one mitt, and the change wrapped tightly in a five dollar bill I dropped into the toe of the other.

"Hurry back, and I'll make us some lunch," she said, giving my scarf one final tug and my back a warm pat as she held open the screen door. I was glad to be getting out. My mother was lonely all the long winter, and happy to have me there about the house, but the holidays were wearing on and I was tiring of her loneliness. I wanted to be outside again, going to school and talking to my friends. But only my father and I had heavy winter clothing which was a luxury then. She had one thin coat, so she had to wait until my father could drive her, or those rare days when the Chinook winds, full of the punky heat of spring, blew down from the Rocky Mountains and turned the streets to slush for a day or two in January or February. Then she got out.

Outside, the road and sidewalk were one thick grey arch of frozen packed snow that crunched and creaked dully under me, as I picked up each overboot with the shoe inside slipping up and down generating a little warmth with each step. My hood was drawn tight over my toque pulled down to my eyebrows, and the scarf covered my cheeks. Only my eyes and my nose poked through the narrow band that remained.

It was eight long blocks to Waterfield's General Store in the cluster of buildings on the main road that ran parallel to the C.P.R. tracks. Through the small slit of my hood, I could see all the way there down an eight block long tunnel of ice and packed snow. For good reason no one else was out today even though only a few more days remained of Christmas holidays. The chimneys above the houses on each side of the long street had tall feathers of smoke rising from them. There was no wind but the cold was heavy and solid. No sounds carried out from the nearby houses and even the creaking of my boots on the snow was absorbed quickly into the frozen air as if I'd never been there.

I trudged slowly like a bandaged-up alien, with the huge boots on my feet and one arm swinging off tempo with the money in the toe of my mitt throwing itself ahead, and the cold began to cut my breath into smaller and shorter gasps. The tears in my eyes had begun to ice and I rubbed my eyelashes with my mitts to keep them apart. My scarf was now thick with frozen breath, rendering it stiff as my mother's laundry clattering on the clothesline in the wind, until she stacked it like thin sheets of plywood in her basket. I pulled down my scarf to take in air which seared my throat. Ice crystals were growing slowly up the drawstring of my hood as they had already on the power lines over my head. The store was still four blocks away: it was now as far back home as it was ahead. I trudged. I felt my brain freezing and I thought of the girl from Altadore and boiling water; I couldn't imagine it hurting at all.

Outside Waterfield's General Store, the Seven-Up thermometer stood with the red line at -23 Fahrenheit and the windows with the Black Cat decals and the huge red Coca Cola saucer were frosted nearly to the top. Inside, the warmth of the ripe banana and chewing gum air was sweet and immediate. Tom Waterfield looked down from his newspaper spread open on the counter and stared over his half-frame glasses on the end of his nose that made him look always sceptical and deserving of an answer like a teacher.

"Cold out there Tom. Come right in and get warm."

I liked Tom Waterfield not just because we had the same first name but because he treated me like we were equals almost, although I knew we weren't. He didn't call me Tommy like almost everybody else including my father.

I tore off my mitts and handed him the note. I didn't really need one for the groceries but you had to be sixteen to buy tobacco or cigarettes or you needed a note. I emptied out the five and change onto the linoleum counter top.

"What else ya got here?" he read, taking down a green can of Export A with the dancing kilted lady on the front. "Two Cream of Tomato. And Chicken Gumbo. One bread. You get that will ya?"

When Tom wasn't busy like today he filled your order and you helped, but if he was busy, you helped yourself except for the tobacco and the candy he kept down behind the counter in a little window. And he didn't tolerate long decisions on whether you wanted one banana bubble gum cigar or ten Mojoes for your nickel.

"No, bottom shelf, *bottom*, right there," he pointed me down the big section of red and white cans that took up most of the canned goods section.

"There ya are. Small Velveeta from the dairy case and that does her."

A small stack of groceries had risen on the counter. We were running low; the last of the turkey soup had run out and it would be three more days before the weekend and my father would be home early enough to take us in the car to the new Safeway on the other side of town.

"That's . . . " he jabbed the figures into the adding machine buttons, pulled the crank quickly three times for the total and tore off the tape, "six dollars and thirty two cents."

He counted out the change on the counter, sweeping it into the cup of his hand.

"Close. Mom's keeping good track of the money. Six fifty."

I was glad. I hated having to take something back because there wasn't enough money and sometimes there wasn't.

"Thirty-three, four, five, forty, and fifty, " he counted, handing me three pennies, a nickel and a dime. I quickly considered the possibilities here.

"One book of matches, please," I said, "And two caramels." This was my tip.

My hands felt all pins and needles and the tips of my fingers burned like *they* were matches. I'd pulled my hood and my scarf down, but still I'd started to sweat and the rough yarn of the mitten cord cut into my neck.

Tom folded over the bag after placing the bread gently on top. I wanted to stay and get warm, but I felt funny waiting in the store not buying anything else and getting all sweaty and itchy.

As I put the bag down by the door the change rattled in the bottom, and I pulled my hood and scarf back up and shoved my mittens into my sleeves. Then I sucked in one last lungful of warm sweet banana air and scooped up the bag. As I leaned on the outside door, I had to shove it open against the wind and the inner door closed securely behind me.

At first it wasn't too bad. The chewy caramel warmed my cheeks as long I didn't have to open my mouth to breathe. But two blocks later the wind opened my sleeves and filled my hood, freezing my hair and raising goose bumps on my arms. I looked back at the big blue panel truck with the block heater cord running into the store. Waterfields also delivered groceries. But my mother was too proud to ask and I was her son.

A bit of caramel squirted out and stuck to the side of my face, gluing my frozen scarf to my cheek. My hands ached. The bag was getting heavier and I shifted it from one arm to the other. As I put it down to rest, tears started down my cheek and I couldn't see our house even after the wind died. Now I couldn't go back; I couldn't go forward.

I picked up the bag and walked a few more feet and put it down again, this time almost dropping it. No sounds came from the nearby houses. No one looked out. I hated my mother. I hated where we lived, this dumb street, Waterfield's. Then the wind started again.

I felt something on my shoulder and heard a muffled sound above and beside me.

"Here, let me." A man in an army parka and a huge brown toque with a pom-pom on top lifted the bag with one hand.

"That way?" he nodded ahead. "I'll carry, you lead."

Hope goes a long way towards warmth. Instantly I felt better.

"Didn't catch your name. Mine's Arthur."

"Tom," I said, picking the frozen goo from my cheek.

The wind gusted again and we shouldered into it. All I could see was that he was tall and thin-legged but his long stride made me throw my boots ahead of me more quickly now and I puffed to keep up with him. The wind dropped and rose again, picking up the thin loose layer of snow off the park beside us. The ice crystals grazed my nose like cold sand and an old Christmas tree rolled down the road like a tumbleweed.

"Woo, whiteout!" he shouted over the wind.

I halted for a moment. He turned and waited, then put his free hand on my back as I caught up with him.

"Best we not stop. Too damned cold." My father always said goddamn.

It had not occurred to me just then who Arthur might be. Out here in the middle of the day. In a snowstorm.

All the men were away at work. Besides he was doing what I couldn't. But as we passed the red fire callbox mounted on the telephone pole that marked our street, I was starting to worry, but I was too afraid to stare, which would mean having to turn and risk falling. I did anyway. What was my mother going to say. One of her instructions had been about talking to strangers. Not talking to strangers. But only strangers who offered candy.

"I can carry it from here." I looked up. All I could see through the thin band of sight I had left, was the toque and the turned-up collar of the green parka that I now noticed was missing its hood. He also had no gloves and he kept shifting the bag from one hand to the other which he warmed in his pocket. There was something familiar about him now that I hadn't realized earlier. Then a chill that had nothing to do with the weather went through my body.

"Don't you worry buddy, I'll take you right home. C'mon, too cold to stop." I could hear the shiver in his voice, but he kept walking.

Half a mile back down the tracks from Waterfield's was an old railway hotel that the Salvation Army ran as a hostel for single men. The hosties, as people called them, rode the freights or the city buses out to our edge of town. Out behind the hostel, on the far bank of the irrigation canal in a grove of poplar, was a hobo jungle where the men stayed when their time was up. Sometimes the police had to go in and get a body and there were always stories of fights and stabbings. Under no circumstances were we to go near the tracks or the canal.

No one sat beside them on the bus. Some people even got up, shoving, cursing and sat somewhere else or stood up all the way home if one sat beside them. Some were old and surly, talking to themselves or singing guttural songs. Others were young and smart-alecky, talking in loud voices and looking right in the eyes of people who tried to ignore them. All of them wore Sally Ann clothing, dark old coats, usually dress coats that looked funny on a bum. Most of them had bad breath with booze on it. And B.O. The bus drivers had to tell them to shut up or throw them off the bus.

One driver even pulled over between stops once, after they all got off at the hostel, took out a rag and began furiously wiping the hand rails and backs of seats where they'd sat.

"Goddamned swine." He'd glared at me. I nodded in agreement, afraid.

As we neared my house I started to want him gone. What if he wouldn't go. I knew my mother would be mad. Somehow I had failed her. I'd needed help.

As Arthur and I turned up our walk, my mother's face was visible in a small clear circle of glass surrounded by a square-edged halo of frost that filled the picture window.

I wanted to turn and tell him, this no longer needed stranger, to go away. This is my house, mister. Thanks but you can leave now. I knew it was too late. Arthur must have seen her first because he handed me the bag and turned away. But my mother's face disappeared from the window, the front door opened and she stuck her head out. I knew she'd shoo this stranger away after what she'd said.

"Thank *god*. I just called Tom Waterfield. I was so worried when the wind picked up."

She turned to Arthur while she took the bag from me and stopped him.

"Thank you *very* much."

Arthur nodded to her and started back down the walk. I was relieved. But my mother stood watching.

"Wait. You *must* come in."

He paused a moment, confused, but then came up the steps behind me, a little too quickly, I thought. Right then I hated my mother for sending me. And even more I hated her for letting this man into our house. I hadn't asked for his help.

"Let me take your coat," she put it over her arm the way she did for good company and then undid my scarf. "You get out of those clothes and I'll put some soup on. What's your friend's name?"

He's not my friend, I thought.

"Arthur." I fidgeted with the toggles on my boots.

"Arthur, I'm Edna," she said, leaving off her last name. Maybe he didn't have a last name and she didn't want him to feel bad.

"Welcome to our home. Tom will show you where the washroom is." My mother was using her best company voice and manners. We usually called it the bathroom.

He spent a long time washing. I went in after he finished and ran warm water over my hands which made the skin feel as if it was shrinking and too tight for my fingers, but it warmed me up fast. I checked the medicine cabinet to see if anything was missing. My father's Gilette safety razor was still there, his chipped shaving mug and fragrant bushy shaving brush. The Noxzema, the Aspirin, the styptic pencil my father used for his shaving cuts and his Wildroot hair cream. At Cubs, we'd learned Kim's Game where we had to memorize a table full of objects, leave the room and then come back to identify what item was missing. I'd never been good at it, but everything looked like it was here. I heard my mother's laughter and when I came out, he was standing in the kitchen doorway smiling and talking to her.

My mother hustled us into the dining room and Arthur didn't say much, but he seemed grateful to be out of the cold.

"You don't have to, ma'am."

My mother seemed glad to have the company and she flew between the kitchen stove and counter and rushed in with a plateful of long fingers of white bread sliced into "dunkers" for the soup heating on the stove.

"No bother. It won't take long at all," she called out cheerfully from the kitchen.

With the wire cheese cutter she slapped thick slices of Velveeta onto the bread and flipped it onto the waffle iron to grill. The margarine sizzled and smoked with each slap.

Arthur still had on his toque and sitting across the table, he looked ridiculous. I wondered why my mother hadn't said anything. I was never allowed to wear a hat at the table. His face was very red and creased but his voice was young, maybe even younger than my father's. His eyebrows were like two bushy blond shelves on his forehead and his grey eyes pierced whenever they looked in mine. Slowly I was warming up, but when I blew my nose, a strange and familiar smell wrinkled my nostrils.

B.O. — body odour. And then the smell of urine and campfire smoke. My mother had warned me about B.O. Good hygiene, she'd say. Arthur had B.O. And B.O. was a hostie smell.

Most of them had the same red face and smelled so bad you tried not to breathe if they sat beside you on the bus. And now one of them was sitting in my father's chair in a stupid toque, stinking up our house and about to eat our food while my mother was treating him like good company.

Then I realized what was missing from the medicine cabinet: my father's old straight razor that he kept hidden behind all his other things. I wanted to jump up and check. Instead I looked down at the bowl of soup my mother placed in front of me. Cream of Tomato soup. I thought of the story of Sweeny Todd our cubmaster had told us one wintry night when we were alone in a cabin at Camp Gardiner. My throat felt bare naked and cold. I swallowed hard.

Arthur had three bowls of soup and four grilled sandwiches. My mother just kept on bringing them and he never said no. I could hardly finish one bowl. After lunch, Arthur got up suddenly from the table and I nearly jumped. He reached for the knife at my mother's plate while she was in the kitchen making coffee. We'd all be dead, I thought. Downed with a dull knife, Melmac plates and bowls everywhere and our throats slit ear to ear like Sweeny Todd's victims and warm blood gurgling out of us like Campbell's Cream of Tomato soup.

"Don't bother," my mother called out, "Tom will clean up. *Tom.*" She seemed unaware of any reason to fear him, this man with my father's razor in his pocket. I could see the rectangular outline of its case lying horizontally in his pantpocket as he stood up.

He stacked the knife on my mother's plate and put them on top of mine. But I knew it was a ploy. I took the dishes from the table out to the kitchen and went to go off to the bathroom. I wondered how to get my mother alone and tell her. And the telephone hung on the wall between her in the kitchen and him in the dining room.

"Take these out to the table will you?" she stopped me with two mugs and a plate of cookies.

"You smoke, don't you, Arthur?" my mother asked from the kitchen.

"If you don't mind." He shifted in his chair as he answered.

Even though my mother hadn't exactly asked me to join them, I wasn't letting him out of my sight. When she came back into the dining room she brought her long cigarette roller, an ashtray and the can of Export A.

"Help yourself to the coffee and cookies. I'll roll us a few cigarettes."

"You like Johnny Cash?" Arthur pointed to the stack of records leaning against the flip top player. She only had *eight* of his albums.

"You too?" she said more than asked, preoccupied with the quick flip of white paper and tobacco into long white pencils that rolled out on the table.

"I like him — he plays mouth-organ good too."

My mother corrected me if I said good when I meant well. But I was more worried about his free hand which rested on the pantpocket where the razor was.

Then my mother evened out the long white cigarettes and reached into the pocket of her house dress. She took out my father's razor, pulled open its case, carefully unfolded the shiny blade out of the ivory handle and expertly nicked each long cigarette into regular sizes.

"That does the trick," she said, "Nothing else in the house quite this sharp." Then she used a match head to tuck the loose strands of tobacco back into the cut ends.

"Don't you tell your father," she said, giving me a conspiratorial nod.

That still didn't satisfy me. It just meant he brought his own knife. I didn't take my eyes off him for one second. But they both ignored me as he held a match out to her. Her cigarette sputtered and flared the way rollies do. She inhaled deeply and then exhaled through her nostrils filling the air with a cloud of thick rich smoke.

"Would you like to hear something?" she said.

"You got *Orange Blossom Special?*" he asked.

My mother slipped the album from its jacket and set the needle onto the record.

It was then Arthur made his move. Catching us off guard, he reached into his pocket. My father's razor lay closed at the other end of the table. We were defenseless. I put my hands over my eyes. This was it.

I heard a spit-wet wheeze and then a low metallic wail. I looked through my fingers. On the table in front of him was a cardboard box with the lettering:

M. HOHNER
MARINE BAND HARMONICA

Great. Sometimes you'd see the hosties out in front of the Cecil Hotel or the Queens with a hat or a cigar box. The odd one was okay; most just made noise.

While Arthur wasn't great, he wasn't awful either. He wailed in the right places, cupping his hands closed and open for the train whistle parts. His Adam's apple bobbed and his cheeks puffed and sucked as he made the click,

click, cluck sound of the wheels. My mother, meanwhile, picked up the coffee spoons and cupped one inside the other with her forefinger acting as a spring and tapped them in the palm of her other hand to keep the beat as she sang the chorus. Actually neither of them sounded bad.

My mother laughed when the song was finished. I'd never heard her sing or laugh this freely with my father. I knew it was wrong, but I couldn't say a thing to my father because if I hadn't needed help none of this would have happened.

"You got any more songs, Arthur?" my mother asked while she poured him more coffee.

Instead of answering, Arthur began to cough, deep racking ones full of spit he wiped from his mouth with the paper napkin from the cookie plate. Each time he coughed, his body rocked forward almost lifting him from the chair.

"Are you all right?" My mother stood over him with the coffee pot still in her hand. We were both worried now. I wondered about my father coming home to a dead bum in his chair.

"I'm fine," he finally said, wiping his mouth and gulping some coffee which seemed to settle him down, "but I better go."

This time my mother didn't stop him. And as he stood in the doorway, putting on his parka, she pressed a handful of rollies into his and gave him a pair of gloves my father never wore. As he turned out the door, he looked at me and then nodded to my mother.

"Bye Tom. Thank you."

After he left, my mother latched the aluminum door as it banged with the wind. I went to the front window and watched him cut across the park towards the hostel. The needles of the Christmas tree jabbed my elbow as I made a squeaky circle in the frost, my finger going round and round until there was a small clear hole. I watched him appear and reappear in the gusts of snow-filled wind until I could no longer see him, this man for whom my mother sang and laughed, and the small opening closed, covered with my frozen breath. In the kitchen, the tap filled the sink with water; the radio was silent, as was my mother who neither sang nor laughed.

Harker's Dam

Only two people knew what happened that night at Harker's Dam in the spring of 1965. One is dead and the other will never tell.

If this were my mother's story, she'd bend it a little, have the rich kid Clayton Foley being driven away in the big Cadillac ambulance that doubled as a hearse, trussed up in a white belted canvas jacket, to the Apollo ward in the big mental hospital in a town north of here called Ponoka. He's in Ponoka now. And that's that, she'd say, having told how his nails grew so long they curled in on themselves, cutting into his hands. His hair so matted and greasy the hospital barber, a man who'd killed, shaved him bald with electric shears.

And my mother would say Teddy Doyle was dead the day his father died. When that explosives plant went up in a boom and a cloud of smoke, she'd say, that cloud carried off Teddy and his father both. That little boy watching that explosion from his school window didn't stand a chance. And everything that happened at Harker's Dam five years later was written on the calendar of destiny in big red letters a long time before. My grandmother tells me the same stories and she lays them open and upturned like the palm of a hand. She says there's another madness, where there's no slips, no accidents — everything is planned. Me, I think it might be part of the truth, but it didn't explain everything that Saturday night when Clayton Foley shot Teddy Doyle at Harker's Dam down by the river where everything was alive and green again.

The television announcer said on the Sunday night news the shooting was an accident, involving two local teenagers, the victim not yet identified and no charges had been laid in the incident which occurred at a local picnic spot late Saturday evening.

By Monday morning, it was all we could talk about as we huddled in small groups waiting for the bell in the schoolyard.

"Teddy Doyle," Kenny Dawes said and shook his head, his eyes haunted by what he'd seen. "And it was no accident — Clayton Foley had a gun," he said to the others. "We were there." Adrian and I nodded, although it wasn't exactly true we'd seen it.

We all knew him. When we got bikes, Clayton Foley got a moped. We got skates, he got a complete Detroit Red Wings outfit. We got gopher traps, he got a pellet gun. Buzz Foley owned the gravel pit and twenty brand new trucks and he was twice the age of our fathers. An Oklahoman, he made his money in the oilfields at Leduc. Some of the others' fathers worked for him, but ours didn't.

"He had a gun," Adrian said, "but that doesn't mean he did it."

"He doesn't go anywhere without a gun." Kenny faced him down.

"Same as when he shot at my old man and me. Point blank," I said, just as the bell sounded. "We were out on the irrigation ditch." The others seemed glad to be free of us and left for class. Adrian seemed irritated. Kenny listened as I talked over the bell while we walked down the halls which seemed a darker and stranger green than I'd noticed before.

"My old man caught him, dumped the shells and threw his gun back at him. He just stood there until we were back in the water and yelled he'd sic his old man on us."

"Not everybody would have done that," Kenny said to me, but my father had a construction job downtown where Foley Transport couldn't touch him.

But it was true, the morning of the shooting we had been down at the dam like we were almost every Saturday. Kenny, with a syrup bottle of water tied like a cavalry canteen to his belt, and me, with my army surplus gas mask bag full of Cheez Whiz sandwiches, set off together with our friend Adrian Carp. The three of us climbed up out of the Ogden flats onto the prairie where the runoff hadn't dried yet on the brome grass and the biggest of the pothole sloughs were still fresh-smelling and deep with ice saucers floating in the middle. It was the time of year when we could take our jackets off for an hour or so only when the sun reached its height near noon. But it was spring.

Harker's Dam was located below the sudden steep edge of the prairie on the outskirts of Calgary, Alberta, between a sharp bend of the Bow River and the gleaming white tanks of the Imperial oil refinery. The crowns of poplars were already greening up under the sandstone cliffs along the river. It was always warmer there, and we spent that Saturday, as we had many others, soon as the snowdrifts disappeared, skimming stones across the current, building a lean-to and eventually a fire as the sun began its drop behind the mountains to the west.

The dam was really just an old road over a backfilled beaverdam across the inlet to an island in the river. The name referred as much to the island where Arn Harker owned a pig farm until the late fifties when his house burned down. But unlike the television said, you had to be pretty hard-pressed to picnic there, with all of the broken beer bottles and the stench of the oily backwash from the refinery. Even the trout we sometimes caught were tumorous and stank of crude.

And while we hadn't exactly seen the shooting, we had seen something else. We were on our way home late that Saturday afternoon when we spotted Teddy Doyle and Clayton Foley coming down the cliffs. None of us really thought much about it then, except that Foley had a gun. It wasn't unusual for him, but it made us nervous and seeing him with Teddy Doyle was strange. Very strange, we'd all agreed. Nobody hung around with Clayton Foley. Later, it scared me to know we'd seen Teddy Doyle walking to his death. I wished we could have warned him, but my mother would say his fate was settled long before and all we would have done is postponed it.

After the national anthem and the Lord's Prayer, the principal clicked the P.A., blew loudly into the microphone and announced: "Sincerely, we regret the passing of Edward Doyle known to most of you as Teddy . . . " clicking off later after the other announcements with a static and crackling finality. He too called it an accident. We looked at each other.

Kenny, as always, sat by the windows at the back, as if ready to leap out and down two stories to escape. I sat in the centre of the room where I could hide from the teacher's questions. Adrian sat up front. An invisible wire linked the three of us who were there at Harker's Dam that day. My mother would say death was something that couldn't happen to us yet. We couldn't imagine it, but we thought we wanted to.

Some people thought the shooting was cold-blooded murder, a rich kid who'd run out of thrills. Maybe. But my mother says there's two reasons that explain everything: money. Or love. And what they don't is explained by madness, which of course just about covers it all. My grandmother says the worst kind of madness is not accidental, but that which is planned, where every detail is covered and the story is perfect, too perfect, and none of it's true but you can't prove it, but you know, she says, you just know. But all I know is what happened next.

Later that week, it would have been about five or six days after the shooting, on a Thursday or Friday, the principal called Kenny down to the office. After he was gone for a long time, Adrian turned part-way around and stared at me — I knew we were next. I tried to focus on the pictures of Bishop Laval and Chief Crowfoot that hung on each side of the portrait of the Queen at the front of the room. Which only got me thinking about Teddy Doyle and how we'd lost him after he started to keep to himself since that day five years earlier. We'd been doing a fractions test in our grade four homeroom. Miss Boyle had up the Mercator map, with the Neilson's chocolate bars over the Arctic and Antarctic, pulled down over the answers she'd written on the board. I remember finishing and thinking how cruel it was that I couldn't ever think of the Arctic now without hungering for Crispy Crunch. I'd heard a funny sort of pop and turned around to see if Kenny'd let one. Then I heard another one, louder and puffier, outside the room. Then the windows on the side rattled. Suddenly Miss Boyle whirled around, snapped down the venetian blind, but not before all of us saw what happened.

Across the schoolyard, past the gravel pit and across the main road, a tall cloud of smoke was rising and starting to drift. We heard several more pops. Teddy Doyle stood straight up in his chair, facing the window, his mouth open as if to scream. But he didn't. Instead he ran out through the coat room into the main hall. We could hear the squeak, squeak, squeak of his runners on the linoleum and then the loud slam of the outside door. Several of the girls started to cry as Miss Boyle told us to get our coats. As we were dismissed, we could hear the siren atop the fire hall begin to wail. Teddy Doyle's father worked at the explosives plant that had just blown up.

As it turned out, we weren't next.

"Bull — shit, only parents and cops would believe a story like that," Kenny said, dragging on the cigarette cupped inside his hand the way his uncle learned in the war so the enemy snipers couldn't take a fix. We all stood out behind the I.G.A. across from the school, hidden in the alley behind the garbage bin, safe from the principal.

"Did you tell them we saw anything?" Adrian looked at him.

"Nope and that's what I would have told the cops even if we had. You guys notice anything about the gun?" He turned to Adrian and me. "Told 'em I didn't see anything so you guys couldn't have either."

"It was a .22 . . . " I said, grateful for Kenny getting us off talking to the cops.

"No shit," Kenny scowled and rolled his eyes. "Foley told the cops the whole thing was an accident and that Teddy picked up the gun and shot himself when the trigger caught on a tree branch because the gun didn't have a trigger guard. It had fallen off. Can you believe it?"

"Where's the gun now?" I asked, thinking how hard my father had thrown the gun. Which might have broken it.

"Obviously," Kenny said, "they haven't got it. Clayton Foley claims he was so spooked he threw the gun off the dam."

"And it was dark, so he couldn't point out exactly where it went in," Adrian piped in.

"How convenient," Kenny snorted, smoke jetting from both nostrils.

"It just might be the truth," Adrian said.

"You know what I think," I interrupted him. "He shot him in the head point blank, just the way he shot at me and my dad."

"Ah come on," Adrian said. "Everybody's shot at something out there and maybe your old man was over-reacting. And besides, there's a big difference between stupidity and cold-blooded murder."

"Yeah, you tell that to Mrs. Doyle," I glared.

Kenny stepped between us.

"What do you think?" Adrian asked Kenny.

"I think we should go find that gun." I blurted out the first thing that crossed my mind.

"Yeah," Kenny said. "Let's get that rich bastard."

Madness, my mother says, causes people to lose control. Their grooming goes first: their hair is unclean, their fingernails uncut. They stop cleaning, stop caring, and it's that, not the wildness, that's madness.

That night, it would have been a Friday, six days after the shooting, we built our camp on the widest, deepest part of the backwash near the dam where we could see anyone coming down the cliff. Behind us were the ruins of Arn Harker's farm, bleached wood and cracked concrete foundations overgrown with wolf willow and poplar. Blackened boulders, charred wood and brown jags of glass marked the fire rings of summer drinking parties. Beyond all this were the woods and through them, the Bow River, running high and cold and dark with glacial silt and runoff from the foothills. It would be another month before all the snow melted in the Rocky Mountains.

We brought sleeping bags and enough plastic sheeting and rope to build a simple lean-to — it wasn't yet mosquito season and it rarely rained this time of year — so one end was open facing the sweet-smoking, high-cracking fire we built of windprunings and driftwood.

Our plan was simple; we'd drain the backwash and locate the gun. Which we all agreed was the key to everything — if it really was missing the trigger guard, then at least we knew that. We figured he'd thrown it in the backwash in front of the dam — if he wasn't lying. That was where everyone camped or partied. Either way, the river was too deep and swift and we needed this one sure thing we could do. At first, none of us had wanted to believe Clayton Foley had done it deliberately: now it seemed we had no doubt, maybe because doubt was too large and uncertain a thing for us then.

"We got an hour of daylight. Maybe." Already it was hazy with dusk and Kenny's cigarette bobbed and flared in the corner of his mouth as he pulled on his gum boots.

"If you guys pry, I'll pull the rock," he said, between puffs.

Kenny Dawes knew all the trails in and out of the river valley, but he was equally at home in a back alley as on the run-down island. He knew all the hidden nooks and tucks below the sandstone cliffs. He could spot a used condom — he called them sheiks — or a tiny brown field mouse, either one invisible to the rest of us in the tall grass that grazed the cliffs and willow stands along the water's edge. He was our guide in the river world with all its decay and splendour.

The dam held back a large pond and was backfilled with boulders dredged from the old river channel, the beaverdam long since rotted, and the narrow top was now loose gravel and mud that formed a rutted trail joining the island and shore. The outside slope was steep and a trickle from a culvert ran into the overgrown channel, eventually seeping back to the river through a rank-smelling marsh.

The inside slope of the dam was shallow and ringed with a greasy collar of liver-coloured mud held back by boulders and the blocked culvert. The pond looked about twenty feet deep, judging from the dry channel behind us. The culvert was just under the surface of the water; it was strictly for overflow. Arn Harker probably watered his hogs here once, but someone had plugged the culvert to deepen the water for swimming or diving a long time ago.

"Shit — it's cold!" Kenny shouted, clapping his hands to keep warm. His pant legs were rolled above his knees and his white socks on a bent willow shone like small matching ghosts in the dusk. His boot tops buckled and water gurgled in as he stepped down, and the oily mud sucked back at him as he lifted each foot. The water in the backwash, though warmer than the river, was too cold and littered with broken glass to go barefoot.

Adrian pulled stones from the dry side of the culvert while I used a long-handled shovel to scoop out the muck and pry up the smaller boulders in front to help Kenny.

But after only a few minutes he came out. His lips were quivering and he shuddered in the cold air. When Adrian tried to put his socks on for him, they both started yelling.

"Jeez-us Ker-rist Al-mighty," Kenny kicked and shook his legs. At first I thought it was the cold.

"Oh god look," Adrian said, disgusted. By now it was darker and Adrian turned on the nine volt spotlight he'd brought from his old man's garage.

"Stop jumping around," Adrian said. Kenny's legs danced in and out of the splinter of light. Several long black globs, runny and slimy like blood clots, were fastened on to the upper parts of his calves.

"Bloodsuckers," I gagged, as if I'd swallowed one.

"Where's your smokes?" Kenny nodded to his coat lying on the ground. Adrian didn't smoke but he lit one anyway, puffed hard and put the lighted end to the biggest of the leeches until it sizzled and curled, loosening its suckers from Kenny's leg. Adrian carefully squeezed it off and flung it as Kenny watched in shock.

Afterwards, Kenny came back from the lean-to, with his sleeping bag draped over his shoulders like he was king of the island and pulling on the cigarette Adrian started.

"Guess we'll have do it from the dry side now," he said.

"Most we'll be able to drain is two, three feet. My old man's got a grappling hook in his truck," I offered.

Kenny crawled into the lean-to while Adrian and I worked away until the spotlight dimmed, clearing only a small opening about the size of a fire hose that unleashed a steadier trickle of water down into the old channel.

The plastic sheeting on the lean-to snapped in the breeze and the flames of the campfire shone upwards through it, casting strange shadows on the trees above us and we could see our breath as we waited in our sleeping bags for the cans of beans and chuckwagon stew standing in the coals. Upriver, the sky above the cliffs was backlit with the glow of the refinery where the lights of the cracking towers blinked like parallel stars and drafts of fresh oil shocked the damp night air, making us giddy.

"Wish we had some dynamite," Kenny laughed. "We'd drain it in no time."

"My old man says someone rolled a brand new Studebaker Hawk over the cliff and it's in there," I said. Our yard was full of cars he was always fixing up.

"Bet there's bodies too," Adrian said. "Like the sacrificial pools in Mexico. Knives and virgins. Gold even." Adrian's mother had a subscription to *National Geographic*. I'd read that issue too.

"Cut it out you guys," Kenny said, "You'll both be havin' nightmares."

All of us knew one thing: Foley was still out there. He hadn't come back to school but the light in his upstairs room had been on when we just happened to be walking up the alley behind his place the night before.

But our sleep was interrupted only once by a car that remained at the top of the cliff, shining a spotlight down along the road and over the dam; cops or guards from the refinery not even bothering to drive down.

When we woke in the morning there was a dusting of frost on our sleeping bags, but the sun soon came over the cliffs and burned off the droplets, some big as grapes, on the inside of our shelter. The early light stung our sleepy eyes.

Kenny made coffee in the bucket-handled coffee pot Adrian had also brought from his old man's garage. He threw in two handfuls of ground coffee, pulverized the shells from the eggs he had frying on the cast iron griddle and threw them in with a dash of salt. We'd brought enough gear and food for a week.

"Cowboy coffee," he said in good humour. None of us except Kenny drank coffee at home, but we all drank it at his house. And when we weren't trying to be Indians, we were cowboys.

"It's gone down," Adrian yelled, as he peed into the backwash.

"No thanks to you Carp," Kenny yelled back.

The coffee was good, sharp and hot, and we made campfire toast with willow switches held over the fire. After breakfast, following Kenny's lead, we washed our cups and plates by sticking them in the mud and pouring boiling water over them.

Around the backwash, the exposed mud had started to dry and flies were hatching and a few stray bloodsuckers lay dying on the shore. A dresser, once white and now grey and without drawers, tilted up out of the water. The rotting wooden-spoked wheel of a Model A lay further along the bank. A car roof rose out of the middle of the water, the corner posts cut, but minus the car. Some people used them for sledding down the nearby hills. Leggy water striders skimmed the surface tension of the pond leaving circular ripples behind them. Just below the filmy surface was part of a sunken raft with an oil drum still lashed to it.

On the far shore, the milky tube of a condom stretched out like a skin shedded on the mud. Nearby, the long handle of an old shovel, as if someone had left it there and was coming back after lunch. Kenny took the condom and fitted it carefully over the handle.

"R.C.M.P. rain hat," he joked, still preoccupied and looking with the rest of us. Nowhere was the gun.

"Shit," he said. "Nothing?"

"The river's still high," Adrian said, "Until then . . . "

He was right — at the other end of the island, the channel was still open and the high water level wasn't helping any.

Glum and aching, we hiked over the island, about a quarter mile across, to check out the river bank in daylight. The far side of the island was barren with ragged banks shorn away each spring by high water and stunted trees cropped by the constant wind. Weathered post stumps and slack barbed wire marked a pasture with trees older than us in its centre. Our feet gathered mud and clicked and sucked on the gravel as we walked along the river bank, the brown gumbo and pebbles making thick Frankenstein soles that we paused every dozen paces to kick off.

"When was the last rain?" Kenny asked when we stopped, poking the charcoal of a fire ring with a diamond willow stick. Kenny and I watched a lot of T.V. at his place and we'd seen this on *Gunsmoke*.

"Week and half, maybe two," I said, knowing what he was getting at.

"These are old. They weren't here," Kenny said, "And no one would be down here at night this time of year without a fire."

Slowly we circled back, under the railway trestle towards the open channel by the oil refinery. The air was heating up and we tied our jackets around our waists as we crashed through the wicked green willows lashing our arms and faces if we didn't catch them in time. The island stank ripely of refined oil, leaf mould, smoky gravel dust and the froggy dead water of the marsh. Our old winter noses crinkled and flared at all this. But the hot spring sun, almost white as it shone over the cliffs, was tiring our search. Soon delirious bank swallows would shoot out of their clay O's in the cliffs and swoop through the chute formed by the greening poplars of the island and the tawny bluffs and gullies of the prairie. Then I thought of all our stuff we'd hauled down, now it had to be packed uphill in the heat.

We had almost circled the island without seeing anything when Kenny spotted it.

"Over here," he pointed, tramping through the bush towards a stand of poplars. There was a fresh fire ring and a large pile of unused driftwood. It had been quickly abandoned. There were large shards of clear glass from wine or liquor bottles.

"Holy shit." Kenny stood in front of a tree. In the soft bark of a young poplar were several fresh pock marks the diameter of a pencil. "They were right fuckin' here."

We gathered around the tree, excited but worn-out and still wary.

"What's this prove?" I asked.

"Nothing," said Adrian, "except that *somebody* was here."

"Yeah, but notice something about these holes?" Kenny asked, "How tall was Teddy?"

Everyone looked at me. I was the shortest guy in our class. Teddy Doyle was second shortest. He and I were usually last to be picked for teams because of it.

"Stand here," Kenny pushed me into place against the tree and picked up a stick, put it to his shoulder and pointed it at me like a rifle. "William Tell, get it?"

"No," said Adrian, disbelieving. Kenny was scary sometimes.

But as I turned around, three of the holes were just above my head, and several others to the left or right.

"You might be right, Dawes," Adrian bit the corner of his lower lip and nodded. He was impressed. So was I.

"Teddy was killed playing chicken," Kenny said. "Look here at the gravel." There were several large brown spots.

"Blood turns brown when it dries," Adrian added.

"They must have been drinking," I offered.

"They had to be piss-ass drunk," Kenny continued. "Look at the glass — that's hard stuff. Teddy was lonely but he wasn't dumb and Foley's weird, but he's no fuckin' psycho."

"Or is he?" Adrian asked. "We should go to the cops, you guys."

Kenny stood in front of him with his head cocked and his chin out.

"With what?" he asked. "They're not going to listen to us. We haven't got the gun. And what if the fucker threw it in the river? They're gonna drain it? His old man's got lawyers — they'll take us apart. *We'll* end up in jail."

"He's right. There's probably dozens of these in the trees around here," I said. All the signs along the roads here were scabbed with rusty bulletholes. And in our neighbourhood, a policeman was *not* your friend.

Kenny wanted to stay another night. Secretly, I think, he liked the thrill of that place, but the warm weather was melting more snow in the foothills and the river was already high and rising. The dam *had* flooded over before.

As we climbed again back up to the prairie, the first true heat of summer stopped us, our necks collared with sweat, the rough webbing of our rucksacks cutting us. We lay winded in a heap of bare arms and aching legs at the top of the cliff. The mud and woodsmoke mingled with our sweat and the warmed earth gave up its first dusty whiff of sagebrush. The quick *screep, screep* of gophers on a nearby mound sounded at us, and a red-tailed hawk glided across the river, wheeling back again and again, then soaring low, its soft *kiree, kiree*, like a running down alarm above us. Our eyes burned with lack of sleep and now, too much sunlight, and we were somehow further apart than when we left two days earlier. None of us talked.

Before us, a pale bent track of spear grass meandered over the open prairie and down the far valley back into town. When we rose finally, each step homeward took us away from what we'd left behind. As we sorted our gear on the cold cement floor of Adrian's father's garage, the voices of the adults called out to each other, irritating and insistent. I knew we'd tell no one — and no one ever believed Kenny Dawes.

Some things don't happen in one day or one night except on television, or in my mother's stories, but something changed that spring at Harker's Dam. First Adrian, and later I, stopped going down to the river. It never seemed to bother Kenny, but then it was his world more than ours.

What was at the bottom of Harker's Dam? I've always wanted to drain a pond or river just to see — like they do at the mall; silver and copper coins, wet and clean, gleaming like minnows, at the bottom of the fountain, startling and naked. Wherever that gun was, it's probably still there.

After that, changes came quickly because the days, each of them brand-new and unsettling to us then, went by like highway miles we wanted behind us in our rush to travel.

The old dam is a *real* picnic area now. The bush is cleared, the lawns seeded and cut; there's a new concrete dam with a paved road over top of it. The pond is smaller now, partly filled in and full of cat-tails planted for the ducks brought in by the parks department. Named for some politician no one remembers, who campaigned to have it cleaned up.

And the oil refinery is gone. The whole thing trucked away, its site a flat wasteland that you pass over on the new freeway quick as a blink. Someone started a greenhouse there a few years back, but everything died. And on the hottest days you can still see an oily rainbow slick seeping along the river. It had always been there, a handsome brute of white tanks, towers and catwalks. Like our fathers, we never thought we'd see that. This was Calgary, after all. Oil was forever.

He didn't leave. Not in a belted jacket, out of sight in the frosted windows of the ambulance. We turned to some new thing and he just went to school somewhere else. And we lost track. I've always wondered — it wasn't money — was it love, was it madness? Maybe not the way my mother or grandmother would have it — but some other kind that just comes and goes.

He's out there, somewhere. And he knows who he is, what he did. He knows.

Bad Eyes

"He's here!" my mother yelled again. I grabbed my hardhat and picked up my gear at the top of the stairs. My mother stood in the kitchen doorway wearing a wistful "my son is a man" look.

"See you later," I said on the run. Bernie's '58 Buick was waiting under the streetlight in front of the house. My first job. I could hardly wait. And my first boss, Bernie Laverty, was a genius.

We knew him because his brother sold us a dog. Purebred Black Labrador Retriever, his papers said. He came with a rich man's name: Daniel Jenkinson III, of Avondale, although he wouldn't answer to anything but a long exaggerated Dan-ny. He also had a bad eye which was how we got him. My father's supervisor was the eldest Laverty, Freddy, who raised dogs and gave us a deal because Danny couldn't see well enough to retrieve in the field trials. The day we got him was the first time I met Bernie Laverty.

While my father and Freddy went in the house to get the cheque, Bernie stayed outside. At first the dog tore around the yard, sniffing everything high and low. When he stopped to drink, I looked him over closely. I'd turned ten two weeks before and he was supposed to be my birthday present. But I wasn't sure if I wanted a half-blind, secondhand dog who wasn't exactly a pup either. Bernie must have sensed this because he took the choker chain and pulled the dog up to me.

"Let him lick you," he said. Reluctantly I did.

"Watch," he said, as he took off his glasses and held them on Danny's muzzle.

"He needs glasses —just like us," Bernie said, as Danny stood there puzzled and serious-looking with glasses on. We both laughed and I was no longer ashamed of my dog.

The Laverty boys, as my father called them, were often the topic of supper if they weren't our guests at it. There were three of them. And they weren't Irish either. Their real name was Tsachnikov. My mother learned they were actually Russian Jews who escaped from the Germans during the war. The old man and his wife fled with their two boys. Bernie was born later in a D.P. camp after the war. When the old man died of T.B., Leah Tsachnikov went to live with relatives in Montreal, married an Irish steamfitter and moved out west. She and the boys took on his name and his Irishness as my mother called it.

The middle one, Johnny, drank and spent most of his time out of jail in the Detox. When his mother wouldn't feed him, mine did. Bernie was the baby, ten years older than me. Even my mother, who was silently tolerant of the older Lavertys, liked him. He was a short handsome guy with wavy black hair and the first I'd known not ashamed to wear glasses. A lady's man, said my father, who liked women himself. And Bernie got his trade ticket in a year and a half when everybody else needed four.

He also played piano, trombone and guitar, and once he got the highest marks in the country for trombone ever awarded by the Royal Conservatory in Toronto. None of the local papers carried it though, because Bernie was in Kingston Pen at the time. He and Johnny went on a bender one night and decided to rob a local rancher rumoured to have a stash hidden in the walls of his cook shack. The old rancher heard them coming and waited with a shotgun after calling the Mounties. When Bernie put the crowbar to the window, the shotgun went off and both brothers ran right into the spotlights of the Mounties.

Johnny walked, on a technicality, but Bernie made good time taking high school by correspondence, and later trombone. Then he started reading law books to help another inmate with his case. Somebody suggested law, so he started a course towards a degree at Queen's. No question about it, we all thought Bernie Laverty was a genius.

Two summers after he was paroled, when I graduated from grade twelve, his brother Freddy offered me a job working on the new insurance building downtown. Bernie came home from Queen's to work each summer and I was to be his helper, starting on the nightshift the first Sunday after graduation. If I liked it, I could apprentice in the fall.

The grad dance was Friday night and when I got up Saturday afternoon, my father called me out to the garage. On his work bench was an old toolbox he'd repainted.

"You'll need this," he said, more to himself than to me, as he put a ballpeen hammer in the box. "And this," taking a hacksaw and pipe cutter from the drawer where he kept his spare tools. Then he got several screwdrivers, some plastic and some wooden-handled, I'd never seen before.

"Flathead, Robertson, Phillips," he listed, not looking up. Names I already knew. After he found a tape and a chalk line, he reached far back under the bottom shelf and brought out an old wooden chest. In it were some blacksmith tongs and wooden-handled pipe wrenches. Still crouched down, he handed me the wrenches without saying a word. They were the oldest tools I'd ever seen. I knew then they were my grandfather's.

Not much more was said, but when I went back into the house and down to my room, on the chair beside my dresser, my mother had placed my father's old work boots and several pairs of his socks with darned toes and heels. The boots were stiff and as I pulled them on, my feet curled into the shape of my father's. The coarse wool of the socks pressed like burlap against the inside of the steel-capped toes that cut into my soft feet. When I walked, my feet tilted outward now with my father's walk, a walk my own shoes had started to wear.

When I went upstairs Sunday morning, there were now two lunchpails yawning on the counter, my father's shiny new aluminum one and his old black tin one with his initials blacked out, both of them with our common name stencilled on the ends. Bernie was to pick me up at ten. Our shift went in at eleven.

After supper I pretended to nap until I heard my mother at the top of the stairs:

"Hurry it up. He's here!"

As I stood in the doorway pulling on my new rawhide gloves, with my hardhat and the boots, and turned out the door with the tools and the heavy liquid weight of the thermos in my lunchpail straining my arms, I was sure that all this made me somewhat more a man. And I hoped that whatever Bernie Laverty had would wear off on me.

When we arrived at the Safari Coffee Shop, Roy McKenna and his helper Al Bjornson were waiting in a smoky booth near the back. Bernie introduced us as I sat down. Roy had worked with my father and Al was a student hired for the summer. After a quick coffee, we went across the street and got our gear. As we rode the hoist up the fifteen floors of the nearly-finished building, from the open cage we could see all the lights of the city spilling along the Bow River from downtown out to the suburbs. At the top, weighed down with tools, we climbed up two smaller floors to a series of stairs and catwalks through the boiler room with its submarine-like tanks, gauges and pressure doors.

"Watch yourself," Roy said, before he stepped out onto a steel beam that ran between the ducts of the huge air-conditioning units. The honeycomb of open shafts dropped seventeen floors to a deep sub-basement. I picked my way deliberately along the beam, my breath short and stinging, my hair already damp under the hardhat.

There had been a fire the week before, started by a welder's torch. Before the job could continue, Bernie told me on the way in, all the scorched insulation had to be torn out and carried down. Then the blackened fan units had to be cleaned.

By the time lunch break came at 3:30 a.m., my arms were sticky with sweat and itching from the fibreglass stuck to them, my lungs and legs heavy from the hot close air of the stairwells and boiler room as I carted out bale after bale of scorched insulation. Bernie sent Al down for Cokes. The cold curves of the glass bottle felt good against my chest and the stinging fizz cut through the thickness of my throat. As we sat outside on the roof in the fresh morning air with our backs to the boiler room wall, the first glint of pink light caught the face of the Rockies seventy miles west. The chilled mountain breeze dried my damp hair and sweat-soaked tee shirt, making me shudder. Steam rose from the open soup thermos at Al's feet and Roy's cigarette flared in the fading darkness. Bernie stood in the doorway light reading work orders, looking more like an architect than a foreman in his corduroy sports jacket and glasses.

For the next several days I worked a power grinder fitted with a large wire brush. I needed both arms and all the strength of my legs and back to hold it steady as it ground the charred metal of the fan housing back to its original sheen. The grinder bucked and spun over the metal with 3000 rpm of sharp bristles sending particles of carbon and metal pitting against my goggles and dust mask.

But late one night I was glad for my father's boots. I'd tired, and I slackened my grip. The grinder spun out of control, bounced and ricochetted off the metal. I caught it just as it skimmed across my boot, stripping the leather and polishing the steel safety cap underneath. After that, I didn't slack off for even a second and I smeared dirty grease on the boot to hide my dumb greenhorn mistake.

Each morning we packed our gear back down the hoist as the day crews were coming in. Sometimes as I walked to the bus-stop my father slowed in his car and asked without waiting for an answer: "How's the working man?" And as I stepped down from the long ride on the homebound bus with my lunchpail and hardhat, everyone else was getting on.

Most mornings I'd skip breakfast and go right to bed and sleep the light sticky sleep of summer, with children calling out in the background of my dreams. Most days my mother woke me in time to shower and eat an early supper alone before heading out to work again.

The nights passed quickly as I settled into the roll of work and sleep. And when Bernie wanted a scaffold moved now, I didn't need Al Bjornson. Even the one pound hammer felt light after the heavy grinder. My feet now had brains of their own for walking on high beams and scaffolds. My father's friends included me in their conversations about work.

But the first Thursday I got paid, I was working with Roy when the company driver brought our cheques and a load of fittings. We heard it first from him. There was a big push on to get the heating system completed by fall, so the office had hired on a new man for our shift. Ron Lapis had a reputation in the trade for punching out his foreman. He was a biker who wore the colours of Satan's Law.

There'd always been gangs: The Dirty Dozen, The Outcasts, The Grim Reapers, and The King's Crew, as well as The Law, each with their clubhouse and their turf. No one thought much about them. But that spring things started that had everybody tense. The morning paper ran it like one of those old serial stories, except you never knew when the next episode would come and this was real life.

First, a rival gang — the police had ideas who, but the gangs weren't talking to *them* — had left a goat's head on the front porch of a house rented by a King's Crew member. Two days later someone tried to torch the house. They also left behind one black glove for the left hand, the type railway engineers or bikers like, with a long wide cuff. Then about three weeks later, a fresh cow's heart wrapped in barbed wire was found stuffed in the rural mailbox of the Crew's clubhouse outside the city. A few days later, one of the Crew was lured outside the clubhouse, beaten and stripped of his colours by two members of a rival gang who left behind a matching right glove, mate to the earlier one. The morning paper was now calling it Summer of the Black Hand and quoted the Crew's president:

"We take care of our own. We know who done it."

Bernie must have known who had been hired, but he didn't say a word. When we went back to work the following Sunday night, the air was charged like it gets after an electrical storm even though Ron Lapis wasn't there yet. No one said anything. No one had to. Bernie sent Al and Roy off to the roof. I was to stay and drill hangers for them in the boiler room which doubled as our office and shop. I dawdled, hoping for a chance to ask Bernie. But just as I'd run an extension cord, the door slammed behind us and without turning I knew Ron Lapis was standing behind me.

The door was midway between Bernie and me. As I turned, Ron Lapis dropped his gear just inside the door. He strolled, one hand in his jeans pockets, the other extended towards Bernie who was leaning over the blueprints.

"Lapis, Ron Lapis."

Bernie finished his reading. Ron Lapis was taller, by a head. And with his long black hair and beard, he looked like an extremely dangerous version of Jesus Christ Superstar who was on all the billboards that summer. Bernie looked at his watch. Mine said ten after eleven. Talk about in the mouth of the lion. Ron Lapis stared him right in the eye and said:

"What time's coffee?"

Bernie turned and switched off the light over the blueprints, folded his glasses, placed them in the inside pocket of his jacket. Removing his jacket, he hung it carefully over the back of the drafting chair. He then unbuttoned his shirt sleeves, carefully rolling them up as not to wrinkle them before he turned to Ron Lapis without saying a word.

Lapis' only reaction was to flick his hair in the coltish way long haired people do, revealing a silver earring. There he stood, six feet and two hundred pounds with the small bent cross of a swastika dangling from his ear.

Bernie stepped directly in front of him, so close that the steel toes of their boots would touch if either of them moved.

"I know who *you* are."

With that he pushed his forefinger into the bigger man's chest, sending him rocking slightly backwards on his heels.

"Do you know who *I* am?" he asked.

Lapis winced. His right hand was out of his pocket and rolled into a fist which held a couple of heavy studded rings.

"Go ahead. But be very sure it's what you want to do." Bernie stood perfectly still.

Each word was deliberate and separate, as though Bernie were in the possession of every letter of its meaning. He neither sweated nor twitched. If his face was unnaturally calm, his eyes were both focused and wild. Pound for pound, he didn't stand a snowball's chance in hell, but he had one advantage — Bernie Laverty was stark raving mad.

"Be very, very sure you want to do this."

Lapis started to raise his fist, but stopped at belt level. Bernie was too close to swing at.

"Even if you win, you lose. If you lose, you keep losing. No matter what you do, *you* lose."

Lapis flicked his hair back again and flexed his fist open and shut. Bernie was speaking lower now.

"Ron, if you've got any bullshit to pull, you better do it now."

Lapis started to blink like someone in that game where whoever blinks first loses. He turned first to me like I was a goddamned referee. Then he looked back to Bernie.

He grinned and nodded. "What'd you want done, Bernie?" he said as he stepped back.

As if this was not out of the ordinary, Bernie nodded towards me.

"There's fittings to hang on the 14th floor. Take Tom as your helper."

Ron Lapis picked up his things. I reached for an armful of hangers, grateful for any movement. My hands had been shaking so hard I was afraid to take them out of my pocket.

"And, one other thing," Bernie said before we left, "Coffee's at one and my crew starts at eleven. Sharp."

It turned out Lapis was a real craftsman, thorough and meticulous as my father, and he expected the same of me. And he and Bernie were alike that way. He could cut metal with a sure hand, often without measuring. He wasn't exactly friendly, but he was courteous enough after that and went out of his way to show me what to do. Turned out he apprenticed with my father. I found that out the day I forgot my tape. He asked me to measure out some reinforcing rod. When I couldn't do it, he said:

"Your old man gave me shit; I'm giving you shit."

When we ate lunch he sat alone, smoking and looking out into the summer night. Bernie didn't show much of anything one way or the other. He was strictly professional and Lapis was always polite with him now.

One payday, Roy asked him down to the Sheraton-Summit for a beer. He seemed a good enough guy, Roy said later, although after a few beers he started getting cockier. But in this town, if a biker drinks alone in a place like the Summit, there's always a couple of rhinestone cowboys ready to make an example of him.

Meanwhile, the Black Hand business seemed to quiet down and then one of my uncles who worked for the Highways called up to say a job would be open in the fall. While I was learning a few things, I wasn't getting any keener on working construction forever. The thought of driving Euclids and Cats had a nicer ring than four years' apprenticeship. Besides, it got me out of the house and I'd always wanted to go up north. I told myself that my dad would be crushed. This was the big crisis of the summer. To go or not to go. For me it was never a question. How to tell my parents was.

Then one morning on the way home from work, I read the headline: "Black Hand Strikes Again!" There was great detail about how the corpse of a black cat had been flung onto the hood of the Crew's '51 Cadillac hearse. Later a left-handed glove was mailed to their clubhouse. The following night the hearse was run off the road and rolled. Both Crew members were in hospital and one lost an eye. The next morning the story headlined as "Biker War Looms".

The Crew's President wouldn't talk to the cops, but he told the paper: "It'll be an eye for an eye."

At work that week, Roy, Al and I talked about it when we could, mostly when Ron Lapis wasn't around. While Bernie didn't exactly encourage conversation, he put his two bits in.

"Small town paper selling copies and a reporter who watches too many late night movies," he said as he walked away.

He may have been right. There was a story every day now and even the bus driver on the morning run kept me awake with his theory, and the weekend edition ran a special feature on satanic cults. There was also an editorial under the title: "When the Glove Drops", insisting there was a pattern to the violence and that it was escalating. But during the Stampede the story was replaced with record attendance stories and pictures of the chuckwagon races, the Stampede Queen in her convertible, Buckshot and his puppet sidekick Benny the Bear at the big pancake breakfast on the Eighth Avenue Mall. Lapis was quiet through all of this.

But the morning of the Stampede parade he helped us. Bernie had us stockpile planks and a scaffold outside the hoist. At seven thirty when we normally left, we set up the scaffold and we all hiked it right down the white line past the courthouse on 4th Street over to 9th Avenue where we watched high over the first crowds starting to line the parade route. Lapis passed on Bernie's invitation to join us, but after the parade started, Al elbowed me and pointed out why. There was Lapis sitting perched on top of a company step-ladder, holding a three year old girl whose blonde hair matched that of the woman in a Levi jacket sitting on the bottom rungs.

The next story in the paper was on the back page hidden behind the classifieds and the obituaries. There had been a rumble outside the Crossroads Hotel out on the Trans-Canada. It was believed to be biker-related, as this was the Law's turf. Apparently by the time police got there the fight was over. By now we knew Lapis was involved, because he came in with a swollen cheek and an elastic bandage showing under the cuff of his shirt. Roy humoured him asking what the other guy looked like, but Lapis ignored him and was sullen the rest of the night.

Then, well after the Stampede, around the end of July, maybe even the beginning of August, a church on the outskirts of the city was broken into. The caretaker found the colours, stolen earlier from the Crew member, nailed over the crucifix and a right-handed glove like all the others curled in a fist on the altar. Tucked into the fist was a black rose. This time only the police would comment, saying that a special squad had been formed.

Maybe Ron Lapis did look scared those last few weeks. Or maybe it was a dark look that made him seem just about anything you wanted. Roy insisted later he knew all along. Al and I looked at each other — he had to say that. But I think Bernie knew more than he ever let on. He'd never say anything, but he treated Lapis almost too nicely.

Around the middle of August, Bernie came around with our cheques. He told Lapis, "You're on days September first, if you want."

He took me aside. "It's your pink slip. If you want to stay on, you have to register with the board within ten days."

All I could think of was four years of reporting to the apprenticeship board, classes at the Tech, and exams.

"What do you think?"

"It's your decision. But if you go, you can always come back."

"It's the old man I'm worried about." I never would have called him that to his face.

"You've got a chance he never had," Bernie said.

My father took it well. Too well, I thought. He offered to co-sign for the '53 Merc 1/2 ton with the For Sale sign in the windshield that Billy McDonald's father had parked at the Texaco. It was in good enough shape to get me up there and around. My mother was quieter. But in our family, people don't talk, they do things. She couldn't say too much anyway because it was her brother, after all, who offered me the job.

Al and I had six days left when the whole damned box of gloves hit the floor. I didn't need the excitement. I'd already packed my bags twice at that point. And my mother bought a secondhand Gladstone bag like her father had in the last picture taken just before he died. He was a railroad engineer and they all had them in those days. We were both embarrassed. Me, partly because I had only admired it about a thousand times in the window of Aizenman's Shoe Store, and I knew how little she'd made running the lunch counter at the Legion. She, because it was about the last time she could do anything for me that I wouldn't do for myself and we both knew it. While I used nearly a whole can of saddle soap spiffing it up, I'd finally figured out that with secondhand stuff someone else had worn through the newness. You didn't have to look greenhorn.

All I wanted now was for the summer to end quickly and quietly.

Then it happened. That night Ron Lapis was late. Real late. Eleven o'clock came, then eleven thirty. Al and I were cleaning up together when Roy walked by and whispered: "Shit's gonna fly. Bet he comes in drunk."

When he still hadn't shown up by lunch and there'd been no phone call, I was beginning to think he quit. But a little after four, we were having coffee outside and we heard the hoist start up from the basement. We heard it stop at the top floor. Bernie stayed cool. Al and I looked at each other. This time I was worried. There was not one but two sets of heavy footsteps on the metal stairs leading up to the roof. A few moments later, two big guys stepped into the dark doorway.

The regulation haircuts and suits said it all. As Roy had told us more than once, the only person who wears a suit at four a.m. is either a pimp or a dick. One of them showed a badge to Bernie and together they stepped into the boiler room.

"Something's going down," Roy said.

"No shit, Sherlock," Al said, a lot more quietly, to me. After the two cops left, Bernie came back out.

"They're looking for him." He held up a business card with the police crest and a phone number on it. Not surprisingly, Lapis didn't show up that night or all that week.

There wasn't anything in the paper the rest of the week either. But Sunday morning, I'd taken the Merc out on the bypass road for a little shakedown run when I heard the news on the radio. It was a ten-second item before the weekend weather. "City police report finding the badly beaten body of a man in a ravine south of the city. Police believe he may have been a member of a city motorcycle club. The victim's name will be released after next of kin are notified."

At coffee that night it was all the three of us could talk about. We each felt sorry for him. None of us could believe it.

"I knew it," Roy kept saying over and over, "All along. Vendetta." Bernie didn't say a word. We took it easy the last few days. There wasn't really enough work for all of us, so Al and I cleaned up while Roy and Bernie double-checked everything. Between thinking about Lapis and driving the highway up north over and over in my mind, I numbed out the passing of those dragged-on days.

Lapis was only the second guy I'd actually known who'd died and the first I'd worked with. I wondered a lot about that. I felt wiser somehow, even though I didn't know him that well. Kenny and Adrian would want to hear about this.

But that was all to change. My mother woke me up as she always did around five that afternoon. It was maybe the last or second last day of work. After I'd showered, she took my plate of stew out of the oven and turned up the volume on the bakelite radio she kept on the top of the fridge.

"There's something on the news you'll be interested in," she said. "Listen."

The announcer's voice was very serious: "At the top of the hour, city police have issued warrants for the arrest of Ronald Paul Lapis and James Michael Holgate, both members of the city motorcycle club known as Satan's Law. Both men are wanted in connection with the death of a rival club member whose body was found earlier this week. Police warn that both men are considered armed and dangerous."

Mom turned the radio down, poured herself a coffee and continued making cigarettes with her wooden roller, dipping into the can of Export A and stacking them like white logs on the cheesecloth-covered table.

"Your father had him here for supper once when he was an apprentice."

I couldn't believe what I'd just heard on the radio. Now I felt dumb. Like we'd all wanted Lapis dead. Which he wasn't. And *he* did it.

"You think he did it?" I asked her as I ladled out another helping of stew.

"Leave some for your father," she said. "He could've." She broke each thought to lick the rolling paper's sticky edge and she tucked it into the rubber pouch, trailed a neat line of tobacco along it, then gave the roller a shove and out popped a long white rollie.

"Any of us could've," she said, as she started another one.

I buttered more bread to mop up the gravy and catch the last stray peas. Through the screen door I could hear Norm Graham's mother calling him, "Noremmm." Norm's pet crow mimicked her loudly calling out: "Orn, Orn." Everything always happened at once. I couldn't believe a guy I'd worked with was a killer.

"I wouldn't have," I said to her. I couldn't think of anyone who would either. Well, except maybe Bernie. Come to think of it, maybe any of the Lavertys.

"Don't be so sure." She stopped and looked at me as I started on my dish of rice pudding.

"Your father was in a gang when he was your age."

I knew a little about this because sometimes when he had friends over and after he'd had too much to drink, I could hear his voice getting louder and louder until my mother closed the door to my room. I kept eating.

"They all wore Zoot suits. Wide, wide shoulders with narrow waists. Big baggy pants with tiny narrow cuffs."

It was hard to think of my father in anything but khaki G.W.G. work shirts or his one blue suit. It was also hard to imagine my parents at all when they were younger.

"What happened?" I asked.

"Me," she laughed. "Oh, they had a few rumbles with the boys from Currie Barracks and they hung out at the Lido Café over on the south side. But they were mostly lonely and scared. Most of them were too short or too young to sign up. Your dad tried to, but he couldn't pass the eye test. He was so shy then I almost had to ask him out the first time."

"But he never killed anybody." I counted out the raisins in the rice pudding, rationing one to a mouthful.

"He could've. He didn't. They didn't. But take young guys like that. Put them up to another gang. And some of those boys coming back from overseas were *tough*. God knows what they'd seen. Things got so bad for a couple of years after the war the police chief even suggested they had to sign a book at the police station so he'd know who they were."

She took the pile of extra-long cigarettes, and with my father's old straight razor cut each into regular sizes. Then with a match head she poked the stray strands of tobacco back into each and stacked them ends-up in the empty can.

"Put them up to another gang and they turn into somebody else. Your dad was like that then. They called themselves the River Street Dukes. Based on a book everybody read in those days, called the *Amboy Dukes*, set in New York. Half the town was terrified of them. If I hadn't met him, who knows."

"What happened to them?" I asked.

"Eventually they just drifted apart. You don't walk around with a wide-shouldered suit with a long gold watch chain and big brimmed hat unless you got company. Most of them married. But they might of gone further if they'd been pushed. They were that proud."

As I picked up my dishes I didn't know what was stronger, the sadness for what I was leaving or the excitement of getting to work that last night.

When I got there, the look on everyone's faces was obvious. They'd heard. And they were nervous. Even Bernie, although he tried not to show it. But around 12:30, he told us to pack it in. There wasn't much more to do, so we headed over to the Safari to drink beer until last call and they finally threw us out at 2:00 a.m. I remember being high on the coffee, the excitement. My hands were shaking so much I sat on them so as not to look like an idiot. While Al and Roy jabbered on, Bernie stayed quiet like he was above all this. Al loaded nickels in the Seeburg jukebox that hung glowing and blaring on the wall of our booth.

Later we helped each other load our tool boxes and gear. As he carried my stuff out to the Merc, I had to ask Bernie one last question.

"You think he did it?"

Bernie looked irritated.

"He's innocent, until proven otherwise."

"No, not as a lawyer."

Bernie set down his toolbox and without hesitating turned to me and stared the way he did at Lapis that night.

"He did it alright. But that's not the point is it? You do something, then you think about it. Maybe. Then you spend the rest of the time trying to live with it. If you have a conscience. And I'm sure he does — if he's afraid, he does. Sometimes the dead are lucky."

As I watched the red taillights of the Buick flare like imitation rockets as he pulled out, I was angry. What he said seemed stupid and obvious then. Maybe Bernie Laverty wasn't so smart after all. Maybe he didn't know any more than I did.

Bernie went back to university in Kingston and I went up to work for a year in High Prairie. I never saw him again after that but I run into Freddy Laverty sometimes at the new Legion when I'm in the neighbourhood. Bernie has his own law firm in Saskatoon. He married a lady who's an English professor. She writes books of poetry and is very pretty, he tells me.

Ron Lapis got life for murder. I followed the story on the radio when I could. The trial moved to Edmonton because of all the publicity. He was paroled a few years ago and after learning how to paint in prison, he makes a living in Vancouver airbrushing fantasy murals on vans and trucks. He came through here one year for the Truck and Van Show at the Saddledome. The local paper did a small feature on him.

A few weeks ago, Mom gave me a box of my old stuff including a picture of me the summer I worked with Bernie.

I'm standing out on the back porch in this dumb striped tee shirt with my work boots on and I'm wearing a geek haircut and those glasses we all used to wear with the black tops and clear plastic bottoms. Dad's standing beside me, avoiding looking into the camera, squinting up into the eaves as if he's trying to decide if they need painting. The picture is a little off centre and out of focus. Mom had to take off her glasses. All my pictures turn out now that way too.

In the box were Danny's old dog tags. We didn't have him long enough to take any pictures. The neighbours kept complaining about his barking while I was away at school. He was too big for the yard and hated being penned up. So we gave him to the eggman. I cried quietly in my room for a couple of days. I went out to the eggman's farm to visit him once or twice. The eggman and his wife spoiled him, feeding him eggs and cow's milk. But there was lots of room for him to run and the nearest neighbour was a quarter mile away. It was all for the best Mom used to say. And then one day Danny ran up the road to meet the eggman's truck. But it was just someone else who couldn't or didn't slow down, and the eggman found Danny in the ditch.

Whenever I think of him, I think of Bernie, and all of us with our bad eyes. I'm not even sure what it means. One of those things that keeps coming back to me. Maybe it's knowing the difference between what we think we see and what's really there, I'm not sure. Anyway, it makes me sad and then I'm angry again. Then again, maybe Bernie Laverty was the only damned genius from around here.

Manitoba Maple

"Suzy, your dad called. Twice," Doug said, as I stripped off my clothes in the front hall, a workday ritual I follow before going straight to the shower to cleanse myself of the grass clippings, stray bugs and pesticide residue gathered during the day's work. The clothes went right into the laundry. Once too often, I've brought home spider mites or mealy bugs in my hair or clothes that made their way into the hibiscus or the grapefruit tree.

Twice. That and Doug's tone meant Dad was drinking again. He'd call and call, sometimes hanging up trying to pretend it was a wrong number. But we both knew who it was. Or he would just show up. If we left a door unlocked we'd come in to find him sitting there smoking in the comfortable chair in the front room with all the lights off and the curtains drawn. Or the doorbell would ring at 2:00 a.m. and there he'd be, a dark outline with the whites of his eyes peering through the screen door. When we were first married, Doug was patient. But now even when Dad was sober, Doug usually said "hello" and then "Suzy" in a tone that let me know.

For me, all of this was sort of normal. When my brother and I were younger, Dad was sober most of the time. But as he got older, he was drunk more often. Not in any obvious way. You could smell it for sure, but it was mainly his eyes. With their rolling glance, sometimes tilted with a bit of a malevolent smirk when he was drunk, or drooping with a woebegone and silent stare when he wasn't. And ever since Mom died we spent more and more of our family time with Doug's parents. Doug had made it quite clear Dad was *my* problem.

I could hear the pipe thunk in the wall behind the showerhead and suddenly it ran cold.

"Shit!" I pounded on the tub bottom with my heel. Doug was making supper and had turned on the hot water tap.

"Sorry!" Then there was a new thunk and the water ran warm again.

Dad's calls always put me in a blue funk. Once after visiting him I pounded the windshield all the way home. When we got in the house, Doug turned to me.

"Next time I'm not going."

How could I blame him?

I'd had to forget a lot of things over the years to forgive Dad. My dad for me is two men. Not drunk or sober, but the one he is and the one he was. Just when I start getting used to the idea of hating him, the man he was sneaks in on me and won't let me forget that day when the vice-principal called me out of my grade two class to go home. We kids all knew what that meant. Most of the women in our neighbourhood had fathers and husbands or sons working in the C.P.R. shops or on construction like Dad. All the jobs were dangerous but construction was more so and better paying. And the wives or mothers or sisters all listened to the radio during the day while they washed or cooked. So as I turned down our street I could see old man MacKenzie's wife peek through her bathroom curtains and snap them closed before she thought I saw her. My mom's friend Coreen was just leaving our house, and across the street Mrs. Taylor swatted her littlest, Derry, who stood with his thumb in his mouth and his head stuck between the pickets of the fence.

"Derry don't suck your thumb and don't stare." He stared anyway and she avoided my eyes but said, "Hi Susan. Derry say 'Hi Susan'."

Mom wasn't there when I got in the house but my dad's sister Nora was, with another of the neighbours, Ivy Dawes, whose son was in the same grade as my brother Adrian. I was already crying.

"Sookie, honey. Honey, it's all right." Auntie Nora always smelled of Avon cologne and cigarette smoke. She bent down and pulled my head to her neck.

"Your daddy had a little accident, but he's all right. We'll go see him when Dreen gets here."

Auntie Nora called us by the baby names we used on ourselves before we could talk properly. Nora was a gusher. She was the only one we'd let do that. She didn't have any kids of her own and we both liked her so much we wondered why.

Adrian took his own good time getting home, but I didn't blame him. More than one kid had come home to a lot worse news.

At the hospital my brother and I stood at the end of the bed with Nora behind us with her hands on our shoulders. Mom sat with her elbows on the extra pillow beside Dad.

Her eyes were red. Dad looked right out of it, like he was sleeping with his eyes open. Mom didn't notice us at first. She looked at Nora, then us.

"Come here kids."

Nora had to guide us forward. We were scared.

Dad had his hands held straight out in front of him as if to push something away or to stop something. His arms were resting on pillows to keep them raised.

"Dad had a fall this morning. And he's going to be all right. But we're all going to have to be very quiet when he comes home in a few days," Mom said, looking mostly at Adrian then at Auntie Nora. I hugged the sheet beside Dad, and Mom put her arm around me as I tried to cover my sobbing.

Up close I could see the stainless steel plates lining the cast that ran under each of Dad's wrists and curved up into his palms to hold his hands upright in front of him. Shortly afterwards his eyes closed and he began to move his lips lightly and silently in his sleep.

"Sweeties, maybe we should go," Nora said, taking charge again. Mom dabbed at my eyes with a hospital kleenex. Adrian was already at the door.

Nora drove a big red Chrysler convertible with plastic seat covers that made us slide forward when we stopped or sideways when we cornered. She was a secretary for some big guy at an oil company downtown and made enough to buy a big new car, which in those days set her apart from any of the women in our neighbourhood. Hardly any of them had driver's licences to begin with. Mom even had to get one of the guys Dad worked with to drive our car home.

Nora told us that Dad had fallen four floors from a scaffold that gave way on the building he was working on. He'd fallen head-first and naturally his hardhat came off. What saved him, she said, was that he used to dive off the Centre Street Bridge downtown. He got a trophy for it once. None of my friends ever believed me when I told them this later because that bridge is really high and the river there is fast and shallow now. But Nora said in those days the river was deeper because of the dam built by the Eau Claire Lumber Company.

Anyway, when Dad fell, he went into a dive in the few seconds on his way down and put his hands out in front of him. Doing a kind of tumbling roll, he tucked in his neck and head as his hands broke the fall. It was a miracle Nora said, but he shattered the heels of his hands as well as breaking his wrists. Thank God he was so strong, she said, or he'd never work again.

If he hadn't stopped his fall, well, I hate to think. Like the Hawkins kids. Their dad was an outrider whose horse fell under the wheels of a chuckwagon during the Stampede. They had to move out of their house and go on welfare and that was the least of it.

"Call your dad," Doug said when I came downstairs. Sometimes I envied his relationship with his parents. They were normal. Neither of them drank. They actually went to church on Sundays. Together. And they didn't preach at us about it. If they called he wanted to call them back right away. While he set the table I called. The phone rang half a ring.

"Hi Dad. Yeah. Everything's fine. They did? That *sounds* right. Where are the stakes? Let me look at it anyway.

Tomorrow morning. I'll talk to you then, Doug's got supper on."

I hung up and sat down as Doug dished up the Texas chili he sometimes makes: lots of jalapeno peppers, beef chunks marinated in bourbon — no beans — all meat with rice on the side. Unlike most guys, he likes cooking, *and* doing the dishes. Good thing. I'm not partial to the domestic stuff.

Doug and I met in college up in Olds. He was an "aggie", a rival, and I was a "hort". Agriculture and horticulture. The aggies were mostly farm kids and males, going back to run the family farm when they graduated. The horts were mostly city kids and female. Both of us were from the city; in fact, we went to the same high school but we never noticed each other then. We met in an arboriculture course both groups had to take. He works for the lands department now as an agronomist and I work for City Parks as a foreman — not foreperson — I'm equal, not different. And besides, I didn't work this hard to get there and have them change it on me. I was one of the first women they hired. And one of the first to get my Class "A" truck licence, pesticide licence and a few others besides.

"What's up?" he asked.

"The Roto-rooter man reamed out the basement drain and pulled out a mass of roots. Chili's great by the way. You know the willow and the maple in the backyard. Sounds like it might be them. Anyway, the city told him they're on his property, he foots the bill if they block the main."

"What are you going to do?"

"I'll go look at them tomorrow. The by-law says he's responsible for any damage even if it's off his property."

Another thing about Doug, why I love him, he's the only guy I know who gets excited talking shop with me. Talking about air pruning, heeling-in or bugs with him makes me positively hot. Most guys don't mind a lady gardener, especially watching her start a lawn mower if she's wearing a halter top. It took me a few tries before I could pull a starter rope without falling out of my top, but the minute you pick up a chain saw or back up a semi — well.

"You need a hand? I could come over after work."

I remembered what he'd said earlier, and I knew he and his dad usually went to the livestock auction and farmer's market near the National Hotel on Friday afternoons. Doug's dad was an armchair farmer too, and after ogling the cows the two of them would come back with huge plastic bags of corn or carrots or chicken parts they'd bought from the Hutterites.

"I'll go. But you can put the tools in the truck. You'll have to take the car tomorrow."

"Is there gas mixed for the chain saw?"

"No. But you're right, it's probably chain saw work. Those trees may have to go and Dad will make a stink about that."

The dishes didn't get done that night. We made love easily, and sweatless, with the windows wide open, the dry wind off the mountains cooling my sun-burned shoulders. The room was hazy with falling light and the lavender's dry sweet scent. Doug's arms were wiry and as he pulled me astride him, I held his shoulders and his neck until I came, pulling and curling him against my chest in my own strong arms.

When he fell asleep, his chest and stomach contoured the hollow of my back, his arm circled my waist. I lay awake listening to the wind. Later I dreamed a variation of a dream I've had most of my adult life. That I'm driving my truck down a long, steep road that ends in a river. I stamp on the brakes again and again, but the road turns to mud and the truck slides below the surface and then I awake into another dream I forget by morning. Sometimes in the dream, I'll be walking, sometimes I'm with Doug, most often I'm alone. Always the road ends in a river. Almost always I cannot stop, but sometimes I can make the truck fly magically through the air and land safely on the other side.

Friday is my usual day off. City Parks works a four day week. And Dad took early retirement about six months after Mom died. The arthritis in his hands and arms had gotten so bad he had trouble holding a cup of coffee some days, let alone a hammer. I pulled our truck up in front of the small white house on the corner lot where my brother and I had grown up. A lethargic green ash planted by the city stood in the front yard and the lilacs gone now to seed covered the window of my parents' bedroom. On one side of the house the peonies were in full bloom and on the other the delphiniums and tiger lilies softened the corners. The kleenex blooms of the hollyhocks filled the space beside the front steps.

All this was Mom's doing. The house was her duty but the yard was her domain. And somewhere along the way I became her assistant — no, her co-conspirator — and we would fill the yard with colour and life in defiance of this dowdy town and the people around us. She instructed me carefully in mowing, pruning, and most of all, in the patience needed to work with living things. She knew a hundred tricks — from how to root the Boston fern by pinning a leaf of it to damp soil, to tying a plastic bag filled with sphagnum moss until roots started magically mid-branch of what would now be a new ficus or hibiscus. Or to coat the blind eyelids of the new-born bunnies or kittens with vaseline when their eyes failed to open.

At first, my brother, two grades ahead of me, and I both did equally well in school but soon I was spending more and more time in the yard, tending either the plants or the animals we acquired. And Mom let me take over each new job as she went on to another. I learned to use my Dad's bench grinder to sharpen the spade and the shears. Eventually Mom got a job downtown at the Parisienne Hi-Fashion Shop with the neon Eiffel Tower out front. She worked there until she got cancer, working up to manager of the ladies' floor. She had an orderly sense of fashion that Adrian picked up. One thing, I sure didn't. My brother spent more and more time at the library. When he wasn't there, he'd have his nose in a book. Finally he landed a job there during high school.

Dad was a shadow man who appeared from time to time, but all the while our lives centred around his difficult presence. I never questioned any of this then. Each of us seemed to find our own way without ever talking about it. And even after Mom died, Dad still considered this yard more my domain than his, as if she'd passed on her special powers to me.

I went around the sideyard and through the trellis gate Dad built. Mom had roses vining over it at one point. I'd given up on the finer points of maintaining the yard. Between our lives and jobs it was all too much sometimes.

Beyond the gate to each side of the garage the twin birdhouses perched on poles with rims of sheet metal to keep the cats down. All of this Dad made from scrap lumber and metal he'd scrounged from buildings he worked on, usually rescuing a load of something on its way to the dump by giving the driver a bottle of rye or a case of beer. The paint was bubbled and flaking on the garage and the birdhouses leaned a bit down wind, another job I meant to get around to. The next two largest trees were actually green spruce that now shaded the garage. Our spruces, which my brother and I received in waxed paper cartons on Arbour Day looking more then like sturdy green feathers than these tall trees that now measured out our short lives.

I'd always liked trees best in my work; they were my area of expertise and that helped in job competitions. Everyone expects the lady gardener to mind the pansies or the begonias but no one expects her to ride the cherrypicker up as far as it goes, climb out with a chain saw to a lightning-damaged crown to prune it back; or to wedge herself into a crotch three stories up, leaning her chest into the auger for balance, hammer in reinforcing rod and then bolt the tree back together in a rough kind of surgery, all the while knowing that a single branch could dust her to the ground. I love the wind pulsing through the tree groaning and creaking as I straddle it. Flowers are cute but trees are sure and sexy in the same powerful way horses are.

"Suzy. I'll be out in a minute." Through the kitchen window screen I could hear him hack and cough before he spit in the sink. Forty some years of Player's Special and Alberta rye.

I saw the City Works Department's orange-tagged stake in the lawn, midway between a maple and the willow that Adrian and I dug up one year on our expeditions down to the river. We had this idea we'd repopulate the town with gophers and willows. We even went so far as to buy army surplus berets and call ourselves the Canadian Conservation Corps or something like that. Mom humoured us by letting us keep the berets and the willow. The gophers went back out to the prairie.

On the other side of the willow the maple, actually a Manitoba maple, rose up through the sagging clothesline with broken pins bobbing and spinning in the wind. Dad had brought it home for Mom one night like Dagwood Bumstead bringing home flowers for Blondie. But Mom sure wasn't a Blondie. After Grade 12 she left the family farm to come out west and work as a chambermaid at the Banff Springs Hotel. She was engaged to the doctor's son back in Perth County and had been accepted at the Normal School in the fall to become a teacher. Dad was working on the renovation of the hotel kitchen. He was quite the card, she told me once, and a swell dancer too, the way they talked then. They were married at city hall in Calgary and seven months later my brother was born. Her family were strict Methodists and didn't want much to do with a daughter who married an itinerant construction worker from the west.

Her father's family had farmed in Perth County around Stratford since the 1840s. Mom loved to tell us about the colours in October; in fact, she used to recite this poem by Bliss Carman she'd learned in school. It was called "A Vagabond Song" and she'd stand up from the kitchen table at lunch and do the hand gestures to go with it while saying the words:

> *There's something in the autumn that is native to my blood!*
> *Touch of manner, hint of mood;*
> *And my heart is like a rhyme.*
> *With the yellow and the purple and the crimson keeping time.*

She'd clasp her hands over her heart and then make a metronome of her arm with her whole body keeping time. And then she'd shake, her arms spread like tree limbs and recite:

> *The scarlet of maples can shake me like a cry*
> *Of bugles going by.*
> *And my lonely spirit thrills*
> *To see the frosty asters like a smoke upon the hills.*

Snapping to attention, she'd make like she had a bugle and continue:

> *There's something in October sets the gypsy blood astir;*
> *We must rise and follow her,*
> *When from every hill of flame*
> *She calls each vagabond by name.*

Mom would finish, by cupping her hand to her ear, like a forlorn vagabond, with his hankie bundle on a stick, who listens for his name.

She'd had elocution and piano lessons when she was younger and none of my teachers could make poems sing like Mom. It's the only one I ever learned by heart. Something I regret sometimes like not learning French. When she died, I searched all over with my brother's help to find a copy and I recited it at the funeral, but without Mom's verve of course. It helped me get through that time, memorizing that poem. And sometimes when my crew gets bored pruning trees in the winter we tell stories to each other to pass the time, or someone will recite a poem by Robert Service like "The Cremation of Sam McGee" or "The Shooting of Dan McGrew" or that dumb poem about "Only God Can Make a Tree". And I'll recite "A Vagabond Song".

My brother used to say it was corny, but at the funeral he cried too. I saw him. She'd tell us about making taffy by pouring maple syrup over the fresh snow outside the sugaring hut. Some summer nights we'd sit out on the front steps listening to the train whistles and she'd say we'd all go out to Perth County someday. I think that part about the gypsy in her soul was true, but I knew we'd never go. Every year she'd get only a letter or two from her mother, and each Christmas one of those family photo cards from her sister who married a real estate broker, showing their squeaky clean family who turned out to be accountants and real estate agents. My brother and I hated them.

The year Mom died I went up to the Caledon Hills to see the colours when I was at a turf-grass conference in Oakville. A group of us had gone on a bus tour. Back home, Mom went in the hospital a few weeks later and I was too choked up then to tell her how right she was about those colours.

The Manitoba maple is a pretty tree with pale green leaves and grey-green branches that whip out at you in a dozen different directions when they're young. A lot of them grow along the rivers or sloughs on the prairies, or in roadside ditches. It doesn't have much colour in the fall and it's a pretty distant relative to its Eastern cousins. In fact, it's listed in the guide of Ontario weeds. But it's wild and durable in its own way and survives the prairie winters.

Maybe it's just my memory, but around that time both Mom and Dad stopped trying. Or pretending to. She went out to work. He stopped bringing things home and seldom came in sober or before midnight. I gardened. My brother became the scholar. And I knew Mom hated that tree.

She never said it aloud of course, but she never mentioned the maples again after that. Or said her poem or told us as she did every October, "Next year we'll go down to Perth County and I'll show you some real colour."

Lies, lies, lies. The loud voices from the ceiling above my bedroom. Doors slammed. Engines racing. Next morning the silence. And that's what it was. Not so much the telling of lies. But the silence. The curb he ran over on the way home. Conspiring in silence. The too-long wait outside the Legion Hall. The unbearable and unwanted pity of all who knew, looking in the car window. My brother and I pretending to sleep so we wouldn't have to look at their faces. I wish I had it in me to hate him.

"You had breakfast?" The back door slammed behind me.

"It's okay Dad."

"Coffee?"

"Maybe later. They mark the curb anywhere?" I wanted to get on with it.

"Over here." He seemed to walk a little more slowly than I remembered.

"Stay there," I said as I sighted up the peg with the two trees and the orange arrow spray-painted on the curb.

It confirmed what I thought. The city gets dozens of calls a week in the forestry department about this. People plant their cute little poplar or willow too close to a sidewalk or foundation. Eventually the trees do what they're supposed to do and grow, lifting and cracking the concrete.

Some, like birch and willow, need hundreds of gallons of water a day. They'll wrap their roots around a water pipe or worm into cracks and actually split them. These two would have to go or Dad would end up paying more than the Roto-rooter man.

I stood by the peg and looked at my dad through the trees. He knew. Anyone who's worked around buildings as long as he has picks up a working knowledge of the other trades. He knew how to read a survey marker as well as I did. He wanted me to say it.

"Your mother loved those trees," he said, looking at them.

I didn't say anything, though I wanted to. I'd have to eventually. But not now.

"Dad, they're right on top of the pipe."

He studied the ground between his feet the way his brothers all do when they're searching for words and then he looked at me.

"We got work to do is what you're trying to say?"

By lunch time, we finished taking the two trees down section by section; first the lateral branches, then the trunks, until there remained two flat fresh stumps, shiny with sap and chain saw oil. Dad helped me where he could, favouring his hands by using the fleshy parts of his forearms to lift the logs into the truck and gathering branches with his arms instead of the rake or pitchfork.

"One thing," my brother used to like to say, "he's always worked. And he never hit us." I never thought that was much of a defense, as if hitting was the only harm he could do, but he did what men were supposed to do — he worked. And if Mom had taught me what to do, he'd taught me how to do it. Once, I watched him show a gas jockey how to clean the windshield on both the push stroke and the pull without wasting any movement. And that is how I learned to work.

With the auger, I bored a half-dozen holes in the centre of each stump and packed them with a goopy mix of 2-4-D, 2-4-5-T, and 10/30 oil to kill the roots and keep them from suckering. I plugged the holes with wood to keep the birds and squirrels from getting into any of it.

These trees are tough. They can sucker from the bottom to start over again. You see this sometimes when the city cuts down trees after a car accident, or on old farmsteads where the shelter belts are cut down and the stumps send up dozens of new green shoots. I can't help admiring their stubbornness. They're not pretty but you can't kill them either; one man's weed is another's flower. Doug says after the Bomb, the cockroach will be the only creature alive. Them and weeds, I tell him: in a world too hot, portulaca or Russian thistle will push through the rubble of department stores.

Inside I heard Dad coughing. He had his bottle hidden behind the Ajax and Mr. Clean under the kitchen sink. The full ones for company stayed in a cupboard above the sink. As I worked, he'd excuse himself for a "phone call" or to check for mail. I stayed far enough away to avoid his rank, pickled breath, but his coughing and horking made me queasy.

Most of the time, I want little more to do with him than absolutely necessary. In fact, I find it hard to be around anyone drinking or drunk. But sometimes when I feel kind of crazy, I'd really like to get drunk. Oh, Doug and I get a little light-headed sometimes when we go down to hear Diamond Joe White and his band at the King Eddy during Stampede week. But I mean pie-eyed.

"You want to get some lunch?"

I could smell his breath and my stomach tightened. I thought of all the lunches we'd had of Maxwell House instant coffee and grilled cheese sandwiches he did on the burner of the gas stove. And he wouldn't take me where he usually went — the Level Crossing Lounge or the new Legion hall.

"I better go. The dump closes early on Friday." Which was true.

"When will we see you again?" he asked, using the royal we. Did he mean Mom, the bird feeders, the house, the trees, everything?

"Give us a call next week, okay?" I knew he'd call before the weekend was out. What we had wasn't love, it was duty. And sometimes it was all I could manage.

At the dump, the truck heavy with cuttings and logs, I pulled on to the weigh scale and the scale operator gave me a stub. The dump sat nested in a shallow valley atop the dry windy hills on the north edge of the city. Clay berms topped with chain link and barbed wire surrounded it. Everywhere was the whitewash of gull excrement and plastered all along the fence were tumbleweeds and green and orange garbage bags that had blown loose.

The truck bounced down to its wheel wells on a washboard gravel road that led to a slippery clay ramp. The ramp dropped down into a bright valley of garbage opened up like a frenzied sort of cemetery where all we once valued was buried in a race between trucks unloading and Cats covering. Doorless refrigerators, two-wheeled tricycles, a crutch sticking out here and over there, box springs sprung out and losing stuffing. A damp rank wind picked up white styrofoam cheesies and spaghetti spilling from the back of a twenty ton hauler beside me, and everywhere were odd but useful things I wanted to take home.

As the flagman spotted me in, I dropped the tail gate and floored the truck in reverse, locking the brakes. Most of the load shot out the back into the trench. The rest perched on the tailgate and seed pods from the trees covered the truck bed. I gunned it in first and the remainder of the load slid out onto the ground. The flagman turned his head sharply as the stinking wet mud spun from the wheels; I had it in third by the time I was back on the ramp, going up.

The scale operator waved me through the gate, and on the road back down into the city the truck needed little pushing to hit 120K and it bounced lightly in the mountain wind that crossed the dry fields of brome grass in front of me. In the rearview, I watched the seed pods whirl in the box. Some of them lifted and sailed up over the road and onto the prairie.

You see them sometimes, a tree far from any farmhouse or grove of its own, a straggler tucked on a shifting river bank or dry creek bed in July and you know how they got there.

How's your dad, people ask. And you just want to shriek; instead, you say fine, just fine. Fine, fine, fine. And no matter what you do, you're going to feel the same way when he dies. Misplaced, maybe a little vague, but with this raw stinking guilt. Which you're going to shoulder until the day you die.

The Many Happy Returns of Kenny Dawes

As usual, he was a half hour late. I was well into my third beer when Kenny, grinning under his ratty ball cap and lugging his army surplus duffle, an older version of the guy I'd always known, swung through the doors like a pony-tailed Sal Paradise from the books we once read. In those days we'd lapped up all the stories. First Adrian, the reader, then Kenny because Adrian had and then me because Kenny had, passing them on like the Hardy Boys when we were even younger. *On the Road*, *Desolation Angels*, *Dharma Bums*, finally coming down like a bad trip to *Satori In Paris*. It was something we could do then — read and read, then later, drive and drive, sometimes for days just checking out the countryside. The miles pouring in over the dashboard cleansed and soothed us. And Kenny could always talk us into the dream of that moment. For a while we were all lonesome travellers, dharma bums on the road to anywhere.

"Hey man, good to see ya, Tommy." Kenny hugged me, dropping his bag beside the terrycloth-covered table. In the greasy yellow light of the National Hotel, the rounders sat at their solitary tables along the window with cigarette smoke rising from among the clusters of beer glasses into the late afternoon sunlight. They watched us and I was glad to have a friend find me here, even if it was Kenny whose arms were pasty and who seemed frail as I hugged him back. I was embarrassed by my own strength, by sitting alone in this place I hadn't been to in years, an east-end dive full of losers. If anyone I knew saw me here, they might think I looked no different from them or Kenny.

Kenny bought us a pitcher of beer and told me of the trip up from Lethbridge. I'd never learned to hop freights, but he had. After a few hours' wait on the edge of town, he'd spotted a northbound freight. He ran from the ditch where he'd been hiding, and across the tracks, grabbed the bottom rung on the ladder of the third engine. Watching for any unexpected stops and the lights of the railway cops, crouched low on the floor of the driverless locomotive.

He thought the conductor riding the caboose saw him, but took the chance he'd not radio ahead to the Mounties. The long trip north across the prairies and over the dry gulleys went without incident though, accompanied only by the rumbling of his stomach as he carried the miles, singing to the low whine of the engine, keeping beat to the clack of the wheels.

The two rectangles of light that formed a square on the cab floor faded and reappeared again and again under the passing clouds. The metal walls and floors made a small room like a cell. With his duffle bag for a pillow and his jacket for a bed, he'd napped with the hum of the engine and the steady lurch of the cars behind it. Peering out the window, he saw the Indus station. He was hungry and thirsty. Calgary was not far off. He would have to jump before the train slowed into the yards of the C.P.R.'s Ogden shops alongside the houses where we'd been raised.

Since his sister left, and his parents divorced, only his mother lived in the old neighbourhood beside the railyards. And now was not the time to see her, he said, taking off his cap, running a hand over his limp blond pony tail now streaked with grey. Even the few old friends gone, most scattered to the west, the Okanagan Valley and Vancouver, a few to the east. He'd head for the east end. There he was safe, he'd have time to think, plan whether to stay or to move on. He jumped the train just past Indus, outside the city limits, and cut across the fields to the road into town.

When he'd called that afternoon, my wife woke me, and when she said "Kenny", I knew he'd gotten out. I was working a swing shift and sleeping mornings, but I agreed to meet him at the National near the farmers' market. I loved my wife, but I knew she wouldn't understand Kenny or want him in the house, and if the truth be known neither did I. If it hadn't been for her sometimes, I wondered . . .

He got a lift in the back of a pickup truck with two crates full of live chickens heading for the farmers' market, which put him right in the east end. Kenny didn't take buses.

The National had changed little since it was built seventy years ago. There were still separate entrances: Ladies and Escorts. The other simply, Men.

We recalled all the hours we'd spent at the farmers' market. He'd always liked the musty smell of hay and horseshit, the auction barns full of comical pigs, goats and kids, heckling auctioneers. He bought a pig there once and brought it home to his mother. He'd been drinking and it had seemed a good idea, until he woke up the next morning to see it tied to the clothesline pole and his mother straightening what was left of her beet patch.

Next door to the hotel the Hutterites had sold chickens and produce from the backs of their trucks, as they still did, bartering and sputtering in German, and strolling about in black polka dot dresses or broadcloth pants and jackets; the women with their kerchiefs, the men with their black broad-rimmed hats. A Hutterite going door to door selling plastic bags of chicken parts had taken the pig off their hands. Kenny traded the Hutterite a bag of chicken for the pig. His mother boiled the chicken for hours and finally threw it out. She hadn't said anything, but perhaps that was the worst, he said.

We didn't talk about the recent past, how he'd ended up in the Lethbridge jail one night after a two day drunk where he'd filled a suitcase full of cash after cleaning out the receipts for the carnival he was working for. He'd headed south on the midnight flight, but Great Falls, Montana International Airport at midnight is not a busy place and after customs opened the suitcase, the Mounties were waiting for him at the border.

All the beer was softening me now and the softer I got, the more Kenny talked and I didn't mind.

It was Rory's father who had first brought them down here. Rory and Kenny followed him through the tall crowds, mingling with the railway men coming off duty, with their oily pin-striped coveralls and Gladstone bags, swinging their brakeman's lamps, their sharp curses cutting through the blue clouds of their hand-rolled smokes. While his old man drank, Rory led him through the flea market and later the war surplus store with its gunner's turret from an old Lancaster bomber. It was still there and as long as we could remember, still for sale. The surplus store was our museum, part of the Saturday world.

Rory and Kenny would drift east, first through Farmer Jonez Carz with the $25 dollar beaters, then into downtown and the Hudson's Bay store. Rory showed him how to conceal their haul, the yoyos, tubes of glue, pocket knives, in his sleeves. After palming each item, he'd raise his arm to sweep the lick of hair off his face. A floorwalker stopped them once and Rory had held out his hands and opened his coat to show there was nothing there, the tubes of glue resting against the upper inside arm of his coat held there by his slightly bent elbow. Outside he'd laughed and splatted a tube of glue against the window of the Bay, the way a dog lifts its leg against a tree.

Downtown was fast and easy then, I remembered. The movie theatres, the crowds, the twenty cent burgers at the Red Barn. Later they were busted for selling horsemeat, but we didn't mind, they were good at the time. We'd all done stuff, usually together, but when Kenny went off with Rory, Adrian and I stayed behind, envious of this new world that neither of them feared.

Sometimes they'd slip into the Strand, watching two movies for thirty-five cents, listening to the doublejack bottles rolling from the back row. Later they'd push past the sidewalk crowds into the pawn shops and try out the guitars, until they were chased out further east by a shopkeeper muttering Yiddish obscenities. Then they'd run back down Ninth, past all the narrow shops with the barred windows, to get Rory's father from the bar.

We finished the pitcher and Kenny bought a couple of pickled eggs from the barman. We walked out of the dingy light into the sun and through the market over to Ninth Avenue towards the grey tower at the base of Centre Street in the midst of new office buildings, some of which weren't finished when he left eighteen months ago. It was good to walk free again, he said. I didn't say anything.

We drifted past the site of old Calgary, the original fort at the confluence of the Bow and Elbow rivers, then down the empty stretch of Ninth beside the Canadian Pacific mainline that ran west through the city. We'd done this so many times when we were younger there was no counting. The parking lots were littered with bay rum bottles. With Kenny leading as always, we veered over to Eighth. The Hungarian café, the Tokay, was still there where we once got roast duck and torte for a couple of dollars, served by the owner, a mad professor in his white coat and spectacles, wild hair sprung out over his ears. He'd sit with us and watch us eat. "Good? Good?" he'd ask, "Tokay mean honey wine in my country." Sometimes, the old man brought us a second helping. "Don't worry, I charge you for one." His son Tamas was in our class.

And always old man Aizenman's shoe shop with the windows full of tired and curled secondhand shoes and beat up Clark Gable leather coats I'd always wanted. This was the part of town to get deals if you didn't mind looking, had a sharp tongue and money on the counter. Jaffe's was still there, the book store run by a fast-talking old Jew. If there was a school book, he had it. But the real sideline was the bin out front of the store, full of old *Playboy* and *Penthouse* magazines, three for a quarter. There was Harry's News, with cryptic newspapers from all over the world, his window full of harmonicas and pocket watches. The owners stood like millionaires then in front of their stores, warming their big guts in the sun, the smoke of their stogies hanging under the awnings. And the Calgary Shoe Hospital with its new leather smell and rows of cowboy boots in whites and two-tones, and alligator and snakehide, and Alf's pet store with a cursing green parrot without any tail feathers perched in the window along with the cocker spaniel puppies smelling of pissed newspaper and cigar smoke. We were tripping now like we used to. Kenny was humming something and the beer and sunshine helped me forget all there was to remember for now.

But on the other side of the street the Atco trailers of a construction company and a crane rising out of the concrete pit marked the new city moving eastward. He couldn't remember what was there once. A poolhall, the Billingsgate fishmarket? Too many blocks of ghost buildings in our minds.

"Don't know, Kenny, don't know," I said, wanting to keep it light.

He stood with his fingers hooked in the chainlink window cut in the plywood around the construction.

"Remember East Village? The coffee houses. Crowbar, King Biscuit Boy?" he said into the fence. I remembered. The fish chowder of the Billingsgate. Endless games of eight ball. How someone had thought they could turn the east end into Yorkville, like the hippy place they had in Toronto. Kenny had a job for a couple of days stamping out leather chokers for a head shop. He liked to show off his record albums with the guys in the band wearing chokers he'd made.

There was no limit here once, he said. For a few dollars you could buy your gear, a meal, a bottle, and follow an old rounder's directions for the westbound: "Da one with the red flag on the hogshead, she's da one ya want, da thru train. Ride the last engine, don't touch nothin', lie low and they won't bother ya. Jump before she hits Coquitlam an yull miss da bulls," he laughed, pulling his cap down over his eyes. That was the first time, he was seventeen. When all else failed, there was another way. If you weren't afraid, he said.

When the light turned green, we doubled back and climbed the steps, pushing through the swinging doors into the bar room of the Queen's. We found a table near the pay phone and Kenny flashed four fingers at the black-tied waiter who promptly banged down glasses of draft. He downed two of them quickly. He flagged the waiter again and we ordered a couple of cheeseburgers.

In the joint, he said, even the cheeseburgers hadn't tasted like cheeseburgers by the time you'd gotten them out of the pile at the end of the food line. Prison food. We both had an old affection for cheeseburgers, even the bar room ones. The best, as far as he knew, were at Stu's Café and Grill on the Princeton highway he'd travelled once, south and east of Hope. No Hope, the hitchhikers called it. For dessert, strong coffee and rhubarb pie. He'd gone through there once after picking fruit in the Okanagan for a season. But more than once he hitchhiked somewhere for something crazier. The beer was beginning to get to him.

He wolfed down his burger. Mine was oozing and after I ate half, I gave him the rest.

"I'm free, man," he said. You never knew which way he was going to go. Drinking with Kenny made me sober.

It was Rory, he said, who had first brought him down to the Queen's. Said there was a room upstairs with the bullets from a gunfight still in the wall. In those days the legal age was twenty-one and they were sixteen. It wasn't really a crime, he said. They had merely been at the wrong place at the wrong time. Two years later the drinking age dropped to eighteen. But it was their first initiation in the city jail. His mother had to come down to get him out, but Rory's old man had told the cops to keep him there.

After that they started running away, the two of them straddling the track on clear days, watching and sometimes listening with their ears to the rail for the long freights puffing up the track south of the irrigation canal. They would idle all afternoon, lying on their backs on the hill above the school, staring past the clouds, into the galaxies that night would reveal, the world a big easy place. Deciding then they'd run away together. Already, I remembered, their friendship known by whispers: Rory O'Connor ran away last night. He made the train to Lethbridge. Kenny Dawes too. But then they'd always been running away, or always about to. Now it was two of them together.

Always it was out to the tracks, down the irrigation ditch or out to the hidden forts and lean-tos of the river. But coming home was usually the same, red-faced, ducking out of sight in the back of the Mounties' car. Rory spent the night in the Cardston jail, after he'd fallen asleep and the railway cops had found him as the train pulled on cars at Fort Macleod. Kenny got away and hitchhiked back. Already, he and Rory known to the teachers and principals as trouble makers.

I remembered sitting in those god-so-long classes, dreaming of running into the yellow skyline, sleeping under clear skies, eating hot dogs, living forever on five fingers, stealing along the way. And with a shiny harmonica playing "Red

River Valley", poking runner toes, rubber black and smelling, into the hot summer fire. Watching Kenny read the steepled hands of the bold-faced pocket watch under his desk, listening for the 2:20 whistle of the dayliner barrelling out of town, trundling over the black trestle, throttle and whistle wide-open, southbound, driving on out of the schoolyard sky, a silver flash heading for the American border, and *Montan*, as the lonesome cowboys sang at the Saturday matinee. We all envied those cowboys and the two of them, and we dreamed of running, but we couldn't stand the shame.

And it had been Rory, Kenny said, who had started the fire on the south hill behind old man Ralston's farm. Driven by matches dropped in the scrub brush, the spring wind went crazy that year, leaving a trail of crunchy stubble, the burn following the tracks out of the city. Rory had been absent that afternoon, as he often was, and when we all saw the smoke from the schoolroom window, we knew. When we came running after school, the fire trucks were still there, parked in the gully at the top of old man Ralston's farm. The old man, in a World War One trench coat, with his white horse dragging a tiller to break the fire near his fence. Out on the open prairie, the firemen fought fire without water, sweeping the flames out with brooms and wet gunny sacks, the pumper miles away from hydrants.

At first the firemen kept us away, but the wind was winning and soon all of us were beating down small spots of flames with tiny jackets and feet. All of us catching some kind of hell later from our mothers. Their black-faced kids, new jackets torn and dusty with smoke and ash. The fire swept under the barbed wire fences around the gravel pit and along the river. All the streets were filled with smoke, the streetlamps coming on early. It was ten o'clock that night before it finally burned out, but the smell of singed prairie stayed until the next rain and even our bedrooms reeked with smoke.

And later Rory said he'd watched it all from the hill, hidden behind a boulder, lying low in the grass, the stink of sage and smoke in his nostrils and all around him.

If old man Ralston knew whose fire it was, he never told. He must have seen someone on the hill. He chased us all come fall and crabapple time, or if Rory on a quarter's dare tried to ride his dumb black bull into the slough. But there was a new sign on his gate:

PRIVATE PROPERTY

TRESPASSERS

WILL BE SHOT

Had everybody been crazy? Kenny looked at me. They were always being chased out of someone's yard. He and Rory understood early the difference between right and wrong: it was wrong to get caught. They had a harder time then figuring the notion of private property; the private places, they were the places to see, they still were, he nodded to me. "Never found a fence I couldn't get over or a door I couldn't pry," he said, his grey eyes looking a little crazy and far away as he reached for his beer.

They were always climbing over the high wire fences of the gravel companies even their fathers hated, those fences that guarded private bridges over public rivers. Once Rory had snuck up on a guard dozing in the sun at the gate that kept cars off the company bridge. The guard had his hat pulled down over his eyes and a rifle lay across his lap like a Mexican federale in a Saturday western.

Creeping up behind him, Rory slipped a small circle of rope around the leaned-back leg of his chair, then crept into the safety of the bushes where everyone waited, watching. He jerked on the rope and the guard was flat on his back, then up stumbling and cursing, eyeing the rope, crashing and shouting into the bush. But Rory was safe underground by then in the dugout they'd built. The guard thrashed and fired a shot in his general direction. Minutes later, a truckful of flunkies pulled up; gravel company heavies looking for potential bridge crossers, chair pullers and other hardened criminals, he said.

The following morning he and Rory and some of the others were called down to the office one by one. The cops asked everyone the same question. Everyone gave the same answer: "No officer. No, honest." The company claimed someone had tried to steal flares and explosives, and had blamed it all on grade six kids; somebody trying to save his job. Rory became an instant hero thanks to eyewitness reports, broadcast word of mouth. Even the nice kids were impressed, liking the bigger-than-life glamour of a renegade in their midst.

The waiter tapped me on the shoulder. Startled, I took four more beers. Kenny counted out his change carefully, but I stopped him and paid. He said he'd have to cash in his government bus ticket at the Greyhound office.

It had all started then. Over the years that followed, they met again, in the downtown jail or Spy Hill, then Rory went off to Prince Albert. Big time, hard time. First it was the guidance counsellor or the principal, later the parole officer: We're here to help you. But you've got to help us. Always a catch, he said.

Theirs were the names called over the intercom, but they were already wise to the questioning, the signing out, the having to explain. Having ready answers, but still not understanding the rules. But they knew the shortcuts, the ways around the rules.

Kenny got up from the table, brushing against a beer glass, which spilled into the terrycloth before I caught it. I watched him fumble with his dime at the payphone, but he dialled the number instinctively, one short turn, two longs, three shorts, and another long. Our old exchange, BR 9. I thought it was his mother's number.

Eight times the phone rang. I could hear that much. Then there was a pause as if someone had answered. Kenny hung up and came back.

He looked at me. "Rory," he said. With that look, I was nearly sober.

"Kenny," I said, "Rory's dead. You know that."

We all knew the story. His sister had called him at the Prairie Dog Inn, where the pushers hung out and Kenny'd gotten a job as a dishwasher. Rory had been in and out of jail and the Detox and he hadn't seen him for over two years when the news came that cold December afternoon, ten years ago. Rory put a gun in his mouth, leaving the phone dangling, the line connected to his mother grounded in the Legion for the night; her son's last words lost somewhere between a shotgun barrel and a P.A. system.

Kenny'd run out of the restaurant and down the frozen alley, with his grease-stained apron flapping at his knees, the cold air tearing at his face and ears, his arms slippery with grease and water. That was the last anybody saw of him. His sister found him three days later in the Queen's still wearing the apron, just two hours before the funeral.

She'd cleaned him up and driven him there but obviously he remembered nothing of the funeral now, or chose not to. In our small community all the grisly details were public news. None of us could ever understand. Like the private conversation in the principal's office next door, but we could still hear the thump of the strap through the wall. Rory was buried quietly, unlike anything he had ever done, in a public grave.

Kenny stumbled to the men's room. I went in after him. He heaved twice. His vomit was tinged with blood. He made a mitt of toilet paper and wiped his face and lips. He was crying. Stupidly, we'd left his bag at the table. It was still there when we got back. He took it and we left the bar. We walked over to the tracks. He'd catch a train east, he said. Inco was opening up in The Pas, he'd heard. If not, he knew someone in Toronto.

"Not here," I said. "Too many cops. Let's go to the edge of downtown. I'll walk you." Into his hand I pushed two twenties, all I had. He took it without looking at me.

Back out on the tracks he found a slow-moving freight, eastbound. I watched as he ran alongside, with one hand on the ladder, leaned back for leverage, keeping the other hand free, and swung up in between the cars. When his duffle bag sent him off-balance, he slipped down between the couplings, and at the last minute with his feet dragging inches away from the wheels, he swung away from the hitch, caught his balance and with both hands pulled himself up the ladder. But this was no train bound for glory, just to the Alyth yards, dropping off boxcars at the warehouses on the spur line. He'd have to jump before it left downtown, before he was spotted. I started to run towards him.

He fell to his knees in the oily gravel, tearing open his pant legs. I went over and helped him up, but he brushed away my hand. He started back towards downtown. Favouring his bruised knees, he limped across the tracks, watching for the railway cops, and I followed him not knowing what else to do. Maybe he could cash in his ticket, get a bed at the Sally Ann, he said. He would try phoning around in the morning. Maybe somebody would be glad to see him. Maybe with news of a job. Maybe he'd get lucky.

Kenny, always knee-deep in water. There weren't many alternatives to playing lonesome whistle, I thought. In winter, ice cracking in mountain tunnels. In summer, grasshoppers splitting on windows. Singing sad songs in the hobo jungles by the sea. Grey blanket jungles. Fools looking for doublejack. Maybe just a glimpse of the end, or just an end, any end.

Kenny slipped away from my side over the couplings of a stationary freight, looking back at me once — he nodded, it was okay. I couldn't go with him. As I turned back, a blue Bronco with two railway cops pulled up in front of me and I knew then I had a lot of explaining to do.

"Where do you think you're going?" one of them said.

"**Y**ou're *not*," Sheila says, "he's your *boss*," throwing her black braid over her shoulder, and lighting up her twentieth du Maurier since breakfast.

"Oh Sheil, he's not my boss. He's the leadhand."

"Leadhand? Sure, soon he'll be *all* hands." She laughs.

"You should talk, Miss Always-at-the-service-of-the-Minister."

"Woo, Miss Low Blow." She arches her eyebrows. "But *what* service it was."

It's impossible to flag my roommate Sheila. Like me, she's an Ontario girl who came out west for easy money, or so we thought, during the boom. Some people here call us the bus people. We joke about finding us a pair of rich cowboys with a big ranch. So far it hasn't happened.

She's from the Ottawa valley and used to work in Ottawa, in government services. She really likes men — as a group. It's the individuals she has trouble with. But you can't like *that* many men in a town that small. So she left.

She's the older woman here at 519 - 16th Avenue South West as they say out here. I'm twenty-two, she's twenty-eight. She's a waitress at the King's Arms over at the Palliser

Hotel and we met in our social work class at the college. I was waitressing too. Then my hours at the Pizza Palace kept getting cut, and my boss kept "accidentally" brushing against me. So, one night I "accidentally" knocked him with a pizza pan right where it hurts. Goodbye Pizza Palace.

Our pal Giorgio, who's also in social work, heard about these cushy government jobs for students, cutting grass for the highways department. Hey, I'm a farm girl, I thought. So we sent in our applications. Giorgio's in like flynn. I get a little letter that says thanks but no thanks. By now I'm desperate, so early one morning I borrow Sheil's convertible, a red relic from her salad days on the Hill, and I roll right into the highways yard, with the muffler dragging and sparking on the ground. All these guys come out to watch while I ask one of them who looks like he knows what he's doing.

"Up there," he says, shy, but kind of cute, pointing to an office overlooking the yard. Giorgio is pretending he doesn't know me, but up the stairs I go.

Behind a door that says Supervisor, there's a chubby guy with greasy blond hair sitting at a desk. His gut pushes up against the desk and there's a plaque with *82nd Airborne* and an American flag on it. Giorgio told me his new boss was a Saskatchewan farm boy who actually volunteered to go to Vietnam. Just like my cousin Pete. My mom thinks I'm hard-hearted — he was reported missing in action — serves him right, I told her. He spent too much time listening to my uncles and their friends go on and on about the war. He just had to go find a war, even if it wasn't his own, and now he's dead.

Bill the boss was tough, Giorgio told me. Half the guys were scared of him.

I wait a moment and when he looks up, I stand right in front of his desk, hold out my hand.

"Mr. Lamont, I'm Deb Chalmers, I believe you got my application." He avoids my eyes. A pussy cat, I thought.

"Well, we're not actually hiring . . . "

"You hired Giorgio Controne last week. I can do anything he can do — drive a tractor, and I know the business end of a shovel. My dad's a farmer, and as I'm sure you know, work is work."

He just looks at me.

"You *were* hiring last week." I look him right in the eye.

I thought I saw a leer in his smile, but I needed this job and he wouldn't be the first guy I'd deal with, if I had to.

"Okay, okay, I could use another helper. Can you drive a Gravelly?"

"Sure, no problem," I fib, but my dad let me drive everything my brothers did. Turned out to be nothing more than a big engine with handlebars and a mower on the front.

But he's *not* the guy I'm going to the barn dance with on Friday night.

Bill sent me out with the cute short guy and his crew. Tom was shy having a woman on his crew, I could tell that. But it was hot dirty work and we all wore cut-offs and tank tops and sometimes the guys stripped to the waist, so after a while, he loosened up. Once or twice, I caught him staring at me, but he'd look away. I kind of liked staring at him myself.

At the end of each week, Tom took us in half an hour earlier to gas and oil our machines. He'd pick up a case of beer and after quitting time, a few of us sat at the picnic table on the front lawn, talking and drinking cold beer.

Sheila has a thing for mountain men. She says the guys out here *are* different, a little rougher around the edges, and blunt as they are — they're honest. Once you get past the shyness, she says, they're wild men. Well, nobody has as much experience as Sheil — most men go crazy over her — the long black hair, the laugh — and she's stacked, as she'll tell you herself. Calls them the girls. She finds a new dress. The girls will like this, she says. Her current guy, John the forest ranger, wheels in from Banff on his motorbike. He's bearded and hairy like a bear. He's tanned all year round and wears an Indian necklace, a beaded medicine wheel, on his bare furry chest peeking out through his open shirt. Gorgeous, smart, but he won't last. She likes them all too much to like one.

Me, I'm looking for one. *The* one. My love life hasn't exactly been spectacular lately. And my old boyfriend Greg keeps calling and begging me to come back home to Beamsville. He took over his dad's garage. He'll never leave. The trouble with small towns — all these people living the same lives their parents did. He wants me to be the woman his mother was, stay home, have five kids and die. Sorry Greg.

Oh, I date sometimes. I hate that word — so *fifties*. A guy from our social work course asks me out. And the professor from our human relations class asked me out once and then I found out about one human relation he neglected to tell us about — his wife. Men are such scum. Then there's Barry the mailman, whose father's nuts about me. I'm not sure Barry is, and I'm not either. So I had to give him back a pile of jewellery he sent me which I didn't want in the first place. For a while it was Matt the gardener — he's sensitive, caring, and a Gemini to boot, double trouble, and just a little too desperate for someone in his life, but I don't get the feeling it has to be me.

Sheil and I took this compulsory humanities course which looked like it was going to be a real bore until we started talking about the mother goddesses. We decided she's the Ecstasy Mother, like the sirens who called to the sailors on the sea — and they got shipwrecked. And I'm the Good Mother as in the good egg, or as in, always the bridesmaid never a bride. But it helps to know this sometimes. If a guy likes Sheila, he won't like me, or vice versa. Though all her guys end up crying on my shoulder.

So when Tom finally asks me out in a roundabout sort of way — a bunch of us would be going anyway — with the Stampede coming up, girlfriends, and wives of the younger guys from work, it wasn't whether to say yes, but what to do when he met Sheil.

Twice the week before he asks me for the address. 519 -16th Avenue, I say patiently. At first I thought he'd forgotten, but through Giorgio I got the impression he hadn't been out that much and wasn't sure I'd still want to go with him. Then, I wondered what Giorgio had told him about me.

Well, Friday came. I'd showered slowly, luxuriating in the expensive Swedish body gel I'd bought. I changed four times trying to decide how to look nicely Western, but not too corny, mixing a silk blouse with a denim skirt and then with jeans, then a checked cotton blouse before deciding on the blouse and skirt. All Calgary goes silly in a nice way this time of year, like Mardi Gras. Last night on Sheil's shift someone even tried to ride a horse into the Palliser.

"Ooh la la," Sheil says.

"Never sleep with the boss." She wags her finger.

"I know, unless you're prepared to sleep with them all, you should know." Sheil's promiscuity is an embarrassment to everyone but her. She also takes great pleasure in teasing me.

"Will the Honourable Member for Mississauga West please stand," she cackles, "and *it* did!"

I'd hoped she'd be gone, but he had to meet her sometime, it might as well be sooner.

The doorbell rang. He was right on time, I liked that. Some guys try a power thing and make you wait. I watched him down the hall through the screen door. I fixed my hair one last time and glared at Sheil: "You, shush!"

In the oval of the screen door, Tom looks like a cowboy picture on someone's mantelpiece. He's lean and brown, and his Western shirt made a checked *V* from his shoulders down to his small waist and compact thighs. The tan cowboy hat, the faded jeans and worn Western boots make him taller than I remembered. His hair and moustache are tinted reddy-blond and he looks every bit a cowboy, not like a bank manager in Western duds, but the real ones who ride the rodeo.

But he just stares at me through the screen. Our hallway was dark and it was still very bright outside.

"Is Deb here?" I thought he was joking, I knew I looked different at work. He's probably never seen so *little* of me, since we worked half-naked.

"Tom, I *am* Deb."

When he came in, his face and neck were flushed pink.

I introduce him to Sheila, giving her a look to tone it down. She was such a showoff sometimes.

"Would you like to join us," he asks her. I couldn't believe it — already.

"Thanks, but I'm back at the bar at eight."

Later he asked me if I didn't mind him asking her along.

"Not at all," I said.

"Sometimes it's hard being alone, especially when everybody else seems to be having fun," he said.

He obviously didn't know Sheil, I thought. But, here was the first guy I'd ever met who saw her that way.

Four bands played that night. The names were unusual, Sundance Saddle Company, Fire on the Mountain, Asleep at the Wheel, and the headliner, Jerry Jeff Walker, and Tom knew some of the guys in the bands. I'd never heard of any of them. He wasn't shy on the dance floor and could dos-à-dos and swing as well as my father used to do when we practised in the dining room after we pushed the table back and stacked the chairs.

We drank a lot of beer, but we burned it up, dancing clear-eyed and happy. Occasionally we formed a square with the others from work or we changed partners for a dance or two, but as the Tennessee Waltz started, he took my hand and leaned into me, and the pearled studs on his Western shirt were hot against my belly through my blouse.

When he drove me home, the lights were on and John's bike was parked outside. In those days, people slept with whoever they wanted and everybody in our class was doing it, or so they said.

Tom seemed a little shy, and for once, so was I. But I didn't want him to go, yet.

"Let's take a walk," I said.

So we walked, down 17th Avenue and through the park. The fluff from the cottonwood trees was a foot deep all across the park, like dry snow. We kicked it in front of us and as the cars sped along the street, it floated in the air behind them, full of light from the streetlamps.

I grabbed an armful and showered it over his head, but it just blew back on my face. He scooped a handful and sprinkled it on my hair and nose.

"Christmas in July," he said.

The following week was my birthday. I tried to keep it quiet at work, but I think Giorgio must have told. At break, Tom took us back to the shop for coffee and brought in donuts for us all, including one for me with a candle on it.

My dad had sent out a jug of his homemade wine, so I invited Tom and Giorgio for dinner that night. Sheil had the night off and she baked a raisin pie. My dad's wine is toxic. Giorgio started it by flinging a spoonful of peas at Sheil. I picked up a scoop of mashed potatoes and parked it on Tom's head. Then we dug into the pie. There was food everywhere.

Afterwards, while Sheil pulled peas and raisins out of Giorgio's and Tom's hair as they stood over the kitchen sink, I grabbed their clothes and threw them into the wash. Later Sheil and I sat with nothing on but big T-shirts and the guys had bathtowels draped around their waists, all of us giggling like nine year olds, staring at the walls covered with food.

Sheil and Giorgio went off to a movie. Tom played the guitar, singing cowboy songs. It's not everybody's taste in music, but it seemed right.

My bedroom was actually the living room of the old house which had been divided upstairs/downstairs. Sheila and I had the main floor and basement, where her room was, and Nola and Jennifer shared the upstairs apartment. They were exotic dancers. Sheil interviewed them for a class project and after smoking a joint with them, she found out they did some things a little more exotic than dancing.

The class listened shocked as Sheila described how they performed oral sex on men.

"It drives men crazy when you hum to them," she quoted Nola. "And it *really* works," she told our class after our professor had warned us about independently verifying our research.

"My boyfriend's personal favourite is 'O Canada'. Lots of low notes," she said slyly.

Most of the time we don't hear them at all, humming or not.

Our living room with Sheil's pot plants, my stereo and our couch, was once the dining room of a proper Edwardian house, and the French doors that separated it from the old parlour now served as the curtained walls of my bedroom.

That night we lay on my duvet as the streetlamps shone through the transom on top of the front window with its prisms and cut glass diamonds. We just lay there, talking and listening to the sounds of the house and the street. First Sheila came in and much later, a cab squealed out, then Nola's and Jennifer's heels clicked on the walk around the house and on up the backstairs. Finally, the house was dark and quiet, and hoarse with talking, we rolled over and over in bed, hugging each other, and kissing furiously.

When the alarm startled us, we were sticky with perspiration and the warm air of morning; we'd fallen asleep still in our underclothes and atop the duvet.

I made coffee while Tom showered. Then he drove us to work.

"Want me to drop you off at the bus-stop?" he asked as we turned into the district where the shop was. Before I could answer, Giorgio's Beetle beeped twice as he passed us.

"Secret's out," I laughed and shrugged.

"You don't mind?"

"If you don't mind, I don't mind," I said.

After work that night, he dropped me off in front of the house.

"Coming back?" I asked.

"Sure," he said, blushing.

Sheila was sitting at the kitchen table studying and smoking when I came in.

"Well? " she says, looking up. "Did we or didn't we?"

We usually poured our hearts out like a couple of teenagers. Self-disclosure, one of our text books called it.

"I'll never tell."

Sheil looked hurt.

"Oh, you *will*," she said a little smugly.

After she went to work, Tom came over and we ate take-out Chinese food in little boxes with plastic chopsticks and we drank the rest of Dad's wine. Just before sunset, we climbed the hill and walked past all the mansions in Mount Royal.

" 'Mortgage Hill', my dad used to call it," Tom said. "He'd bring my friend Adrian and I here for drives on Sunday and we'd sometimes see all these other people like us in their Pontiacs or their Ramblers gawking at the big houses. 'All paid for by the poor people,' he'd say, waving at them all as they drove by, but they'd look away."

" 'Poor people,' that's what my dad said *we* were." I looked at him.

"The premier lives there, I went to high school with his son. See that one over there with the turret, I had a crush on a girl who lived there. Four cars and only two people in the family drove. She wouldn't even look at me."

"I never felt poor in high school. I was vice-president of the student's council. When I was seventeen, I was crowned the Peach Queen and rode at the head of the parade in a convertible all the way to the fairgrounds. If I'd heard one more old lech say, 'Nice peaches . . . ', I would have decked him."

Tom laughed at that.

"I came in second in our school in track and field. Even played second clarinet in the Legion band. Yeah, I drove Dad's pick-up to school; half the guys thought it was cool compared to my girlfriend's Mustang. But when I graduated, I got left behind. The universities I wanted were too expensive. My parents put everything into the farm."

Tom put his arm over my shoulders as we stood overlooking the city.

"Let's be poor together," I said.

Part way home, a breeze came in from the mountains, full of rain that spotted our T-shirts, and before we got back to 519 a cloudburst flooded the gutters and smacked clouds of dust in the dry yards as we ran. We undressed and lay on the bed, with the window open, smelling the wet grass outside and listening to the raindrops get smaller and smaller. I pulled up the covers, and as we held each other, I felt secure for the first time since I was a little girl and I used to hide under my covers with my cat.

Tom soon fell asleep, exhausted. His chin was tucked against my back, one arm under my pillow, and the other over my ribcage. I lay awake watching him as his breathing got heavier and deeper.

Next morning we laughed as I massaged his arm back to life.

For another three nights, we kissed and rolled around in bed and we talked and talked. Or actually, I did most of the talking, he did the listening. I made us sandwiches and we sat up in bed with the lights out, eating and watching the sky through the transom. Then I asked and he confessed he hadn't had a lot of girlfriends. He was embarrassed about that. Actually, I liked it and didn't push him. But I began to wonder how long we could do this.

The following night was payday for both of us and we went out to dinner, his pick, my treat, to one of those Calgary steakhouses where they serve your meat on a board. When we got home, I sent him off to bed alone. In the bathroom, I put on a night gown, an ivory satin one, with a sweetheart neckline and teardrop sleeves, like Rita Hayworth might have worn. Like her, I'm big-boned. I bought it a long time ago at an antique clothing sale, thinking I'd save it for my wedding night when Greg and I were still discussing those things.

The timing seemed right that night. Whatever magic there is in old clothes, old houses, I'd always believed in it. 519 was my idea. I'd fallen in love with the caragana hedge, the old wooden house with its fading canary siding and white trim, but most of all the transom above the window of what became my bedroom.

And I've always believed that glamour was an old magic women worked on men. That night we made love for each night we hadn't, twice over. The first time, I burst into tears, and Tom held me, not asking, not puzzled, nor impatient. We stayed in bed all the next day and the following. We rested during the day, interrupted only by Sheila's coming and going. We were both too shy to face her, and only after she was gone, we came out to get something from the fridge, the two of us standing in front of its cold light, naked and giddy. Three times we watched the darkness fade and return in the glass shapes of the transom. Monday morning we made love in the shower before work.

After work, he dropped me off before going to his apartment to change. Sheil could tell right away. My eyes were sleepy, but my face was flushed.

She threw her arms around me like we used to do.

"I knew it," she laughed, but as she hugged me, I could feel the tears on her cheeks. When Tom came over later, she hugged him too while he squirmed and blushed. Sometimes I could kill her, but I loved her like a sister.

Tom has never admitted it. Macho pride, and I allow him that. Pride is what shields our wounds. But I knew all along I was his first. And secretly, I liked it. All the men I'd ever dated wanted me to be one. With one or two I pretended and regretted it. Later, even when they knew I wasn't, they wanted to know if this was the first time I'd felt this or that. But it didn't seem to matter to Tom, perhaps he knew it was no blessing.

Anyway, after that very first night, he never did go home again. Sheila got her own place and we rented another old house in Sunnyside, across the river. It wasn't quite as magical or as big, but it was ours. We lived there for a couple of years before we finally married. My father was scandalized at first, but eventually he got over it. He and Tom are so much alike except Tom is a softer man in most ways, maybe because men can be now.

I dropped out of social work and went to work in a boutique. I didn't have the heart for it. And as I told Sheil in one of our fights, I just wasn't selfish enough. Most of the people in our course were in it for some need of their own. I'd found my cure. And when Sheil graduated, Tom and I went to the convocation. She became a case-worker at a halfway house for ex-cons. The guys loved her. Who wouldn't have? She's still not married, maybe she'll never be. I think she likes being a full-time goddess. And she tried to get Nola and Jenny into a program for women.

Before Tom and I moved out east to live on my parents' farm, we went back to 519 to take a picture, but the whole block was gone. The house, the caragana hedge, even the number didn't exist anymore. There was a huge hole surrounded by plywood. A condominium was going up, but it's never going to be the same again.

Tulip Soup

Just before midnight, I parked on a side-street by the Welland Canal where we'd all agreed to meet and spotted Paul Muzzo's van parked in the shadows away from the streetlamps. The other three walked from their vehicles hidden on another street. Only the cold clap of our boots gave us away as we converged on the van. It hadn't yet snowed, but the air was chilled and snappy.

Besides the Dutchman, there were two other guys from Water Works: one I didn't know, about fifty, grey haired and hefty, and another, named Joe Keeler, about my age, thirty-two or so, bearded and quickstriding, a picket captain I remembered from the strike rally. The Dutchman, the old guy and I got in the back. Keeler rode up front beside Paul — and under his arm, he carried a gun case.

The Dutchman looked over at me, while the old guy squirmed in the middle; none of us saying anything. The strike had turned rotten, but no one mentioned guns when we were ordered to report for night duty.

It was a weeknight in early December, when most people having to work the next morning were home in bed. That is, all except the drivers, labourers, and gardeners like the Dutchman, and the secretaries, of Local 749 — On Legal Strike — our sandwich boards said, as we shuffled for the past five weeks in the cold rain or sleet each day, and we paused only to warm ourselves, in front of the steel drums of burning wood, or at the donut shop a block away, our hands curled around the hot mugs in some kind of prayer.

We drove to a quiet district near the freeway, a neighbourhood of wartime houses where the workers from the line at G.M. or the steel plant lived, houses not unlike any of ours.

"Cut your lights. This is it," Keeler motioned to Paul, as we turned on to a side-street where most of the lights were out and only the flickering of television screens could be seen in a few windows, some framed with Christmas lights, others hung with evergreen wreaths. I thought of Deb asleep in our bedroom in her parents' farmhouse. The last five weeks had turned me around. I did not tell my wife anymore about the days or nights on union business. I wanted nothing more than the strike over.

"Okay, stop here. We'll do this quickly and quietly," Keeler said, as the van stopped just short of a streetlamp. He pulled an old pump action Cooey out of its case, took a handful of shells from a pocket and gave them to me and the shotgun to the old guy. I wondered just how quiet a twelve gauge Cooey was on a residential street at midnight.

"You load it. You hold it. You fire," he said, to me, the old guy and the Dutchman, who by luck of the draw sat beside the sliding door on the passenger side. It could easily have been me, the new man, firing the gun, and that's what it was, luck of the draw that night. And the one man among us who didn't own a gun was going to fire it.

My hands shook some, but not as much as the old guy's who held the gun on his lap. I could smell the gun oil in the rank heat of the truck. This was an old hunting gun, well-kept, likely passed down. My father'd had one like it once.

I could also smell the liquid courage on the old guy's breath, but he looked as if he were about to cry. The Dutchman's face was grim in the dim light coming in through the windshield as he stared at the steel barrel which lay across his lap while I shoved in the shells. And it would have taken a greater man than me to back out now.

"It's the four-by-four right there," Keeler said to the Dutchman, as we drove slowly towards it with the headlights off. "Blast him once, just a warning — the fucking scab." He turned to Paul Muzzo, "Then we mat it."

The Dutchman took the gun, rested the butt on the floor, and shucked a shell into the chamber — all with his left hand made strong by years of planting tulips and trimming trees — and with his right, flicked the safety, and gripped the door handle, ready to spring.

Deb and I drove in from Calgary that May to work on her parents' farm, our truck loaded with everything we owned, first crossing the prairies and then winding down Highway 69 through the rock of Northern Ontario and into the south where the land levelled out under the green umbrellas of the fruit groves and trained green rows of strawberry fields and vineyards, singing every Neil Young and Gordon Lightfoot song we could remember.

My wife was happy to be home, calling out view points and telling me little stories she knew. How we beat the Americans in the Battle of 1812. The burning of Niagara-on-the-Lake. About Laura Secord and her cow, how they slipped through the Yankee lines to warn the Canadians. Being a farm girl, Deb liked that, a girl and her cow, fooling all those solders.

The sign on the Q.E.W. to Niagara Falls and Buffalo said "Welcome to the Garden City". At first, I'd wondered why, when nothing but the sprawling General Motors plant and the white tanks of a refinery were visible from the freeway. The air was damp and green and close after the dry open foothills I'd lived in all my life. This place that had seen hard times, I thought, as we passed the rusty brick boxes of the wartime factories and the Lightning Fastener plant on the edge of downtown. "They're famous for their zippers," Deb said, the way people do who know a place. But as we drove on through to the farm, the old town around city hall was as pleasant as old towns anywhere in the east, with chestnut and maple trees arched over the streets, and a large park with an old-fashioned bandshell.

That first summer was humid and hazy and all too hot for me. We both put in sixteen-hour days cultivating and harvesting, our hands stained with the colours of the crops we worked, changing as the weeks passed, from the red of strawberries, to the itchy green of tomatoes, to the furred yellow and crimson of peaches. But soon we closed the window in our bedroom that had been wide open since June.

Early in October, City Hall took my application. There wasn't really enough work on the farm once the fall crops were in. The late apples were almost off and we needed the money. Our savings had drained steadily since we left Alberta that spring, despite the small wage her parents gave us. Besides, I was no farmer and there was a tension between her dad and me.

The woman in Employee Relations said with my experience I'd probably be best in Sanitation either as a driver on the trucks or as an equipment operator at the landfill. They weren't hiring full-time until spring, but if I wanted, there was an opening now as a casual driver to the head gardener in Parks.

A week later I reported to City Works, on Geneva Street, a cinder block building across from the ball diamond in a newer part of town.

Inside the front office, a sharp-featured woman in a suede jacket was eating a muffin at her desk. Down a long hallway behind her, I could see truck bays and City workers. I looked at her and then at the men out back.

"I'm the new driver for Parks," I said. "I was told to report to Earl Sykes."

She looked over my jeans and boots as she brushed a crumb off her jacket with a Kleenex.

"He's out back," she said.

As I turned to go down the hall, she stopped me.

"You can use the front entrance today, but from now on, you have to use the back," she said. "The front office is off limits to the workers."

"Thanks," I said, "But I'll use the rear entrance. From right now on. Have a nice day." The door closed behind me. Later, I found out we were in the same union.

The Works yard was filled with tractors, graders and trucks, some already idling, and inside the building a line of men all in the same blue coveralls was punching in at the time clock. A thin pale guy in black-rimmed glasses and a white shirt was giving orders to a small group of men. Another guy stood on the edge of the group, blond and gangly, looking detached until he spotted me. I stood out in my plaid shirt and jeans.

"Cor Van Reekum —Cory. They call me the Dutchman," he said, as he walked forward, nodding to the group and held out his hand. "I'm the head gardener," he said, with a slight Dutch accent, as he steered me towards the time clock. "You're the new driver."

"Tom Grogan," I put out my hand, barely matching the strength of his. "Where can I put this?"

He took my lunchpail. "Get yourself a time card and coveralls from the S.S.O.," he said, pointing to a wicket with a sign: Safety and Supply Office. "Our's is the three-ton out back."

Out in the yard, a G.M.C. stake bed with a trailer was waiting, already loaded with gas cans and leaf blowers. The Dutchman sat in the passenger side of the cab reading work orders as I pulled on my coveralls. Just then, a Jeep lurched out of the yard with the tailgate open, leaving bags of fertilizer scattered along the road, and a minute later, it screamed in backward, and the same pale guy with glasses I'd seen earlier, jumped out and threw the bags in the back, and raced off again. The Dutchman grinned.

As I got behind the wheel I said, "I was to report to Earl Sykes."

"He just left," the Dutchman said, shaking his head.

As we did the rounds, the Dutchman showed me the city and introduced me to the labourers who took care of the parks and cemeteries, mostly in the old part of town. We dropped off gas cans for them and picked up bags of leaves piled on the curb for composting. At coffee time we headed to the Uptown Café near Montebello Park. Several City workers were sitting in the back when we got there. One of them came over to sit with us.

"Our new man," the Dutchman said to a stocky guy with a labourer's dark tan.

"Hey, I'm Paul Muzzo, shop steward for Parks." He held out his hand.

I introduced myself. Muzzo was loud but friendly and leaned close when he spoke as if each conversation was a potential conspiracy.

"You're from out west, eh? Why'd you leave?" he asked. "It's great with the boom on out there now."

"Couldn't afford it," I explained, "Boom sure didn't help my wife and me. House prices are three times what they are here. Then we lost the right to strike. Essential services they called us. All of us — from the nurses to the guys who swept the government parking lots." They listened quietly. Muzzo looked at the Dutchman and then shrugged at me in agreement.

The three guys at the next table were quiet and I stirred my coffee again. "We'd be fined and jailed, if we struck. You guys didn't hear about this?" The Dutchman and Muzzo said nothing. "Anyway, Alberta got rapped by the U.N. Worst labour laws in the free world." I held my coffee spoon between my forefingers and paused, "That is, outside of Alabama and Mississippi. You won't read that in the *Globe*."

"It's okay, I'd've of left too buddy," Muzzo nodded, "But I hate to break it to you, this guy tell you?" The Dutchman shook his head. Muzzo continued, "Our contract's up end of the month."

"They're offering five over three — we're asking eight over two. Look's like we're walkin' — they're using the G.M. layoffs to screw us — but we *can* count on *you*, can't we?" Muzzo looked me straight in the eye and winked.

Great. I thought the Dutchman had been friendly enough but a little guarded. The next table was waiting for my answer too. They were all union people here, checking out the new man, probably wondering if I was some goon who'd help break the strike. I didn't blame them either.

My father was a union man, forty years, nearly all his working life. And twelve years for me since those first meetings at the Labour Temple on 11th Avenue and before that, the union Christmas parties where my father dressed up as Santa Claus with the smell of rye in his cotton batten beard. Even he complained to my mother sometimes about the politics, but to me it was simple. All the times he was laid off or laid up, the only presents we got came from the Salvation Army, or the union. Back then, my father worked six days a week — sometimes twelve hour days if a push was on to finish a building — blind with exhaustion when he got home. In those days, the union was fighting for a forty-four hour week. They won it eventually, and management automatically took a shorter week too. There was only one answer to Paul Muzzo's question and they didn't have to blackball me.

"Sure," I said, putting my spoon down on the table.

"I'll get your card. Dues are ticked off automatic," he clapped my shoulder. "Better go — here comes trouble," he said softly and motioned with his eyes to the door behind me, "The Slimey Limey." The other table got up to leave too, and as Paul Muzzo pulled on his aviator shades, I could see the twin reflections of Earl Sykes in the mirrored surfaces.

"Morning —Earl Sykes," he said in an accent I couldn't quite place, Yorkshire maybe, as he sat down opposite me. "Grogan. There's a good British name. The Dutchman here showing you the ropes?" He said it nicely enough but the Dutchman bristled. And I'm sure he got the point too. And I wasn't British, not the way he meant, but I let it go.

"Sure is —pretty town here —sure different than where I'm from," I said, doing my best dumb-ass good-ole boy routine to change the topic and knowing the other guys would be watching to see if I suckholed the foreman. And actually, I was only one generation off the boat from Glasgow.

"Whereabouts?" he asked, distracted, taking a pill from a container in his shirt pocket, gulping it down with a coffee while he lit a long-cut Belvedere. The light overhead reflected dully in the bald spot between the two slick wings of hair over his ears. The Dutchman excused himself and went out to the truck.

"Cal-gary, Al-berta," I said, with a drawl we used sometimes out west among family or friends when we were fooling around. An old Scottish name I wanted to add.

"Never been there," he said, taking a long pull on the Belvedere. "You and Hans Brinker will be working together till freeze-up — then you're on snowplough duty. Any questions, you answer to him," he nodded and tapped the Dutchman's place-mat.

"Fine by me," I said, chewing on a couple of choice Gaelic curses I'd heard my grandmother utter after the snotty English vicar had visited.

"See you at the shop," he said on his way out, leaving a half cup of coffee.

"What's his problem?" I asked after I got back in the truck. "Ignoring the fact that he's English. And I'm not, by the way."

"I know. He was the backhoe operator at the new cemetery. A very good worker actually." The Dutchman had more grace than I would under the circumstances. We'd passed the cemetery on our rounds, a barren place with miles of headstones and little else. "One tree in the entire place — and he hits it. Going too fast. Took two trucks to pull him out. He's been," the Dutchman tapped his temple, "Ever since. He took it on the head."

"And he's foreman?"

"He's no gardener foreman — he stays out of my way. Figures I'm gonna get his job and he's right. If I wanted it. Once he ordered a truckload of manure from a farmer — his brother-in-law — and dumped it in the rose garden behind City Hall." The Dutchman raised one eyebrow at me. I looked blank.

"If you don't compost manure — it's full of weed seeds," he explained. "It took six men and a week to dig out the roses by hand."

"But he's foreman?" I persisted.

"He's slightly useless, but keen," the Dutchman chuckled. "City Hall didn't know what to do with him. He couldn't drive backhoe anymore — the doctors had him on medication — so they made him foreman."

"He union?" I asked, wondering what to make of the silence when he walked into the coffee shop. On some jobs foremen are union, others they're not.

"Technically he is — but you saw — we won't get *his* vote. And watch what you say, he takes everything back to City Hall."

The rest of that day, I loaded leaves and clippings while the Dutchman trimmed the hedges along the road outside the cemetery. He worked quickly, without stringing lines, but the top was level and bristled solid as a hairbrush, the sides angled up sharp and clean, slightly narrower on top, he explained, to allow it to grow. I jogged to keep up with him. He only looked gangly when he stood still.

Just before lunch, we took a load to the dump and on the way back stopped by his house. He came out with a thermos full of soup, and a lunch of sandwiches and fruit salad. He kissed his wife on the way out and she waved to me. She looked about twenty-three, not much more; a soft woman, with brown bangs that reached to her eyebrows and highlighted her chubby cheeks, and her belly was huge.

"She's beautiful," I said, as we drove back to the cemetery. "And due very soon."

"Eight weeks," he said soberly.

"First kid?" I asked.

"Third. I got a boy, two, and a girl, four."

"Well, at least your sperm count's good," I joked. But the Dutchman didn't laugh.

"Not a good time for a strike is it?" I said, thinking the same thing myself. We'd planned on being in our own house by next spring. Our house money was disappearing fast, without any hope of getting it back. That was all I could think, wondering why we ever left Calgary.

"It never is. Let's go in here," he said, as we pulled off to eat lunch in the shade of some weeping willows by the

Welland Canal where a laker passed Lock 3, downbound for the open waters of Lake Ontario.

Two weeks later, at our Tuesday night meeting, Local 749 voted 83% in favour of a strike — that included the Dutchman and me; Muzzo was right, the City offered us nine percent over three years. Standard contracts were two years and they were trying to change the rules. The local hadn't gotten a raise in four years. But it all sounded good in the news and the mayor, a former golf pro, went on television to say that a million people were out of work and we were lucky to have jobs. That was one way of looking at it. The local's president called a strike rally for Friday night, on our last working day.

That last day on the job was one that we would have gladly paid to work. Despite the cold November mornings, by midday we'd find a place away from the road where we could work with our shirts off without any taxpayers phoning City Hall. The last of the scarlet and yellow maple leaves lay plastered on the windshield. Things were so quiet downtown, we could hear the throaty horns of the lakers over in the locks. The Dutchman and I spent the day planting tulips in Montebello Park. We were both in a jovial and fatal mood, and the Dutchman made a confession.

"You know, I've always hated tulips."

"That's like a Scotsman hating porridge," I laughed.

"In Holland, during the war, the Germans stole everything. My mother and father were starving. Finally, they dug up the tulips and boiled them into soup. My mother never allowed them in her house after the war. And I can't plant them now without thinking of what bitter soup they must have made," he said, tamping bulbs into the soil with

TULIP SOUP 137

the heels of his hands. Across the park I could see Earl Sykes' truck hidden where he thought we couldn't see him.

The U.A.W. hall out on Upper's Line was smoky and hot. Cardboard jack o' lanterns and cut-outs of witches and black cats from the Halloween dance still hung on the wall. All the folding metal chairs were taken when the Dutchman and I got there, so we stood against the back wall. The secretaries, including the one I met on my first day, sat grouped at the front. As she looked around the room she made a nervous smile at me. Like the rest of us, she was worried. The strike deadline was now Sunday midnight with no hope of a late-breaking offer. But that night more than a few were ready to take the city's three-year contract. I was thinking about it myself and I knew the Dutchman was too. Both the union and the city wanted blood — our blood.

The meeting started quietly enough. The treasurer, a wheezy guy in wire-rimmed glasses, stood up to say we'd get twenty-five dollars a week strike pay, while the shop steward from each department went around with clipboards ticking us off. All of us looked puffed up and scared, reminding me of a poultry farm I'd visited with Deb's father, just before capons were loaded onto the semi that would take them away forever. When Paul Muzzo found us, he nodded and checked us off. Finally, when order was called and the noise settled, Ted Kelly, the local's president, took to the podium. Behind him, Canadian and American flags, and the crests of the U.A.W., Teamsters, and our own union, hung from the ceiling.

Kelly was a short, punchy Irishman who'd started as a grave-digger, one of the worst jobs, when he immigrated, then went on to become a leadhand at the water treatment plant. He fixed his dark sharp eyebrows on the crowd: first across the hall, then from the back to the front, and finally the middle, before he spoke.

"Sunday at midnight," he started low, "Local 749 walks. And when we walk, we're goin' to show 'em that we, Local 749, have the balls to stick it to 'em."

The Dutchman looked over at the secretaries and then at me, lowering his eyes slightly. Kelly's choice of words was interesting, but a group of younger guys cheered and shook their fists in the air.

Kelly paused.

"The City's made us an offer, thinkin' we'll take it — but that offer, brothers, is an insult. They're countin' on three things to force us back: one, the layoffs at G.M. will scare us; two, Christmas is coming and we won't go out; three, the weather is on their side."

Kelly paused again, looked around the perimeter of the room before his voice picked up pitch and speed, "But they've forgotten a few things, brothers — who will operate the salt trucks, who will drive the snowploughs — who will patch the frozen water mains — and who will answer the phones?"

He looked across the front row for effect and continued, "Who? The mayor?" Most of the crowd, even the secretaries, laughed at that one. The only jobs the mayor ever had were playing golf, and politics, which some people said amounted to the same thing. Several of the picket captains sat to either side of Ted Kelly, applauding and prompting us. They were enjoying this.

"So, when we walk on Sunday night, and we will walk — remember, they're countin' on us backin' down, as we have the last four years. Yeah, it'll be Christmas soon and yeah it'll be cold. But one good snow storm and we're gonna shut this city down!" He pounded the podium with his fist and the strike captains got up and started to clap and chant, "Strike! Strike! Strike!"

"Let's get out of here," I said, as we got our duty sheets and went outside. "His whole strategy hangs on the weather."

"Yeah," the Dutchman said, shaking his head, "But remember, he's all we've got."

My father always said that when times were good, if he didn't like a foreman or a boss, he'd throw his tools in the back of the station wagon and go on to the next job. Right now I didn't like the boss, and Ted Kelly was a boss just like any other I'd ever had, but I couldn't pack up and leave. And I knew I'd better keep my thoughts to myself out on the line. The Dutchman was right, he was ours.

The first week, Muzzo, the Dutchman and I were part of a roving squad that picketed outside City Hall, City Works and the landfill site, each under a different picket captain. Most of us wore light jackets, and at first, there was a dark good humour on the line, and a bakery owner brought over a box of coffee and donuts each day we were at City Hall. Even the cops seemed apologetic; *their* contract was up next spring. Most people smiled or honked at us as they drove by. This was a union town — they'd been here.

The second week though, things turned bitter, starting with the weather, with a gale cutting in off the lake. It got colder and colder, and there were sleet storms, but it still didn't snow. The last laker cleared the locks, racing down to Montreal before the Seaway iced in and most of us were wearing snowmobile suits on the picket line. And we knew, as long as it didn't snow, the City supervisors could manage on their own with salt trucks. One of them said on a radio program that everyone was pitching in. "There's no complaints —just like when there's a war," he said, "everyone helps."

Near the end of the third week, things really started to come apart. The pilings along the lake were capped with ice like frozen chessmen as I drove in along the Q.E.W. for line duty. The weather kept getting colder, but with sleet that turned to rain in town. There was no way we could keep dry or warm on the picket line, and people going by avoided looking at us.

Then, I'd had a fight with Deb over money. The Dutchman's wife had the flu and he was worried she'd lose the baby. He'd asked me for a loan so they could get a sitter for the kids. I knew it must have been bad —he was proud, and for the head gardener to ask the new man. But I didn't have kids and that made all the difference. When Deb found out, she was furious because she had to take a housekeeping job, which included cleaning toilets, for the owners of a winery in Niagara-on-the-Lake. She wanted me to take something part-time and her dad was bugging me too. I wouldn't, strike pay was lousy, but I'd be scabbing, even if I could find something. And it had been nearly three weeks since we made love and I woke up some mornings breathless and aching, with Deb sleeping on the edge of the mattress.

Paul Muzzo came home to find his wife sitting in the middle of the living room floor, crying, and surrounded by bills. She'd lost her job because of the slowdown in the city.

And then we started hearing stories. Somebody had spotted Earl Sykes and a couple of other foremen slipping into the Works building before dawn. Some of the guys from Sanitation had gone over to a private contractor and were working nights hauling City garbage. Much as I hated them, I understood why they'd done it. But the scab company had been after the City contract for years and we'd heard there was Hamilton and Buffalo mob money behind them. And until something happened at the sewage treatment plant one night, I thought they were just stories.

That bitter night in the first week of December, the Dutchman and I, along with six others, were picketing the gate of the treatment plant when a scab truck roared down the entrance road. Three of us stood in front of the gate, as he dumped the brakes and we saw a City supervisor riding in the cab. The heat of the radiator and the lights on the big Mack warmed our faces. On the radiator cap was a lunging chrome bulldog. A secretary from City Hall, an older woman, hopped on the running board, hung on to his outside mirror and tried to talk him into turning around. Whatever he said, she spat on him, and he shoved an aluminum baseball bat in her face. She lay there in the frozen gravel, her glasses beside her, momentarily stunned. One of the younger guys helped her up and all of us pounded the truck with our signs. But the driver rolled up his window and refused to look at us. Then a police supervisor, who'd been watching from a distance, came over in his cruiser and led the scab truck through our line. He threatened to charge us if we retaliated. But when we asked about charging the trucker, it was an accident, as far as the cop was concerned.

With Christmas two weeks away, the weather cold but clear, and no new offer forthcoming, Ted Kelly called another rally. This time, the crowd was smaller, but angrier, and the local had split.

The younger men sought revenge, but some of the older ones wanted a vote on the last offer. The secretaries wanted back too, but the younger guys were angry.

"You're not the main income in your house lady. I am!" one of them yelled when a women spoke up.

"We've got single mothers here, young fellow," the secretaries' steward said, as she faced him down. I recognized her as the one who'd been knocked down by the trucker a few days before.

A few of us, like the Dutchman and me, were in the middle, but I knew we'd been out too long now to back down.

Kelly had to pound the podium to bring order.

"We're goin' to negotiate at the table, but we're goin' to break their hand under it," he said. "We need strong action. We're prepared to take that action now. Tomorrow night you're goin' to get a call. Then we move on 'em." The crowd hushed as he continued, "When that call comes, you be ready."

"Ready. Go!" Keeler said, but the Dutchman's feet were already running before the van stopped in front of the four-by-four.

Through the tinted windows of the van, it was like watching old black and white television. The Dutchman ran around the front of the van, raised the gun to his shoulder, ten feet back of the pick-up, and let go, smacking out the back window. The shot, surprisingly, wasn't loud, but blunted in the cold air, and the van was already rolling as he jumped in, handing me the gun, its barrel warm and the smell of cordite strong, and before the sliding door closed, we were around the corner as porchlights started to come on.

Keeler zipped the shotgun back into its case, and out on the main road we could hear the sirens of police cars. The Dutchman rubbed his shoulder aching from the kickback of the gun. None of us said a word, and Paul Muzzo circled the block twice before dropping us off.

On the picket line the next day, there were rumours. The house we'd visited belonged to a supervisor in Engineering who'd been pushing for contracting out City work. A scab company truck had burned. Earl Sykes had his house "air-conditioned" — a brick through every window — on the coldest night so far this year. After the picket duty, the crew went off to the Mansion House for a drink, but the Dutchman and I went to Lou-Lou's to get away from the crowd.

"Really taught Sykes a lesson, didn't they?" I said, as we drank our beer. The Dutchman looked embarrassed — this was the last thing on his mind. His wife was okay, but due any day now. He spent most of our coffee breaks on the phone talking to her. I envied him that greater worry.

"What'd his wife and kids have to do with this?" I asked. I was ready to turn in my union card, but the Dutchman stopped me. But we were out of control. We'd gotten simple. It was all black and white, us and them. Rage makes it easy to see simple.

Two days later —just before the union's kids' Christmas party — we settled. The mayor met with Ted Kelly and a media blackout was imposed. The City agreed to stop using scab labour and offered us five over two. That worked out to half a percent a year and the right to a contract we had in the first place. Five weeks for half a percent. How hard it must have been for my father, if this was what we had to do for half a lousy percent. I was starting to understand my parents and what they'd lived through. Ted Kelly and the mayor went on the six o'clock news shaking hands. By then, I wasn't sure which one I disliked more.

And just before Christmas, my mother-in-law answered the door when a union rep brought around a turkey and a cello-wrapped basket of plum pudding, cranberry sauce and shortbread. When I got home, I hid the turkey in the bottom of the deepfreeze and left it there until spring. I told Deb we'd eaten enough crow for now.

Cory Van Reekum's daughter was born on the third of January. She was fine, and it was the best news that long winter. The snow came finally, after Christmas, and all through January and February, so I worked as much overtime as I could stand, putting in sixty-hour weeks, trying to catch up. But it was my choice.

That spring, I got a transfer to the dump and to full-time. I didn't have to talk to anyone, foreman or union, unless I wanted to — the job was pretty obvious. If it was garbage, level it and bury it.

But on the way home some nights, I'd meet Cory for a beer at the Mansion House, and drive past the tulips we'd planted. All those idiot yellows and reds — almost to spite us — like flowers on the grave of something not buried, not dead.

Snake Island

"Go Suzy, you'll really like it," my brother's wife said. Adrian is proud of Lucia, and their house, the little courtyard full of wisteria with a canopy of grape vines, around the corner from the Italian cafés. He "made" dinner that night. We'd stopped for cappuccino, got a roast chicken at a Portuguese place and some fancy breads and dessert from a café where the owner was happy to see him, and flowers from a Korean greengrocer who had buckets and buckets of lilies and glads inside his store. Everyone knew Adrian, and I got the royal tour. We even stopped to see his barber, who's also an opera buff.

My husband insisted, "You can stay over and it would be great for you both." Ice-fishing in February wasn't my idea of a great time, but Doug was tied up at a conference at the Royal York and my brother and sister-in-law's swank duplex in the Annex was giving me cabin fever. Lucia and I got along well enough, given we are as opposite as you can get. She's a smoky-voiced brunette who's nursing supervisor at St. Mike's. And a city girl, with her black leather pants and silk blouses, born in Italy and raised right here in this house. But I felt too outdoorsy for the snazzy leather chairs and glass tables with glass knick-knacks. My brother had definitely married up. They even had a Group of Seven on the wall.

The next morning, after Adrian finished teaching at the college, we took the freeway north over to Highway 48, up through farmland towards Lake Simcoe. The climb out of the congested city passed through rock cuts, the first rough edges of the Pre-Cambrian shield, past groves of leafless sumach and birch and stands of cedar growing wild — something we'd kill for out west. In the mirror, I could see the dirty cloud that hung over the city drop behind us, and up here, the sun was bright and the sky as blue as I'm used to. Snowdrifts filled the ditches and in places blew across the road, but the sky stayed clear. Gradually, the traffic lightened and by the time we were on the regional highway, my brother seemed to enjoy driving and we both sank back into the leather seats. His big Volvo glided up and down the hills and he looked over at me as he switched the electronic overdrive and zoomed ahead when we passed. He was getting roly, his gut tucked against the steering wheel like my father's. I thought of the cars Dad brought home from Farmer Jones. Like the Boat, a Lincoln with huge black fins, and cans of oil and steering fluid under the hood that topped up automatically. Mom made him get rid of it and buy our first and only new car, a Rambler.

"You miss the prairies?" I asked.

"Forty below — the *dry cold*? Carrying enough stuff in your trunk to start a homestead in case your car breaks down?"

"But it's so gloomy here."

"Sometimes. But I come up here, or go up north to Lucia's parents' place in Muskoka."

"You sound so Toronto — *up north*. You're still way south of Calgary. Where's Thunder Bay, if this's up north?"

"It's been good to me, Suzy."

"Never thought I'd see the day you grew your own grapes. The man who used to make Kraft Dinner and Wonderbread sandwiches . . . "

"It's not bad with extra Cheez Whiz, and not half as bad as *your* favourite, brown sugar and butter. Now I'm hungry!" he laughed.

After stopping for lunch at a converted grist mill, we drove on up to the ferry dock to Snake Island, so-named my brother said, as we parked outside a coffee shop, because it was long and skinny. The island, marked by distant groves of white pine, basswood and maple, was barely visible across a wide white expanse of frozen water. My brother used a pay phone in the coffee shop. Everyone here was Ojibwa, he'd told me. Ten minutes later, a van with wide tires pulled up off the lake and beside the Volvo.

"Hi John. My kid sister, Suzy. John Redcanoe. My landlord." A good-looking, rugged man in a huge plaid bush jacket winked at me and grabbed my suitcase. My brother rode on a milk crate, amongst the ice-fishing gear and a chain saw and some gas cans.

"Sister? Your *wife* know about this, *Gee-maw*?"

"Rich white man," Adrian translated, laughing, "but not after taxes, John."

"They call me that too and I'm from here . . . " John turned to me, after making a long swipe with his finger pointed up in greeting, as a truck with another native driving passed us on the ice.

"Yeah, yeah, John. He owns half the island," my brother yelled.

"I worked down in the city, bought a Mustang —moved back home five years ago — I was a case worker in the courts. I'm trying to get this guy to move here before he gets more grey hair."

We followed the ice road, through drifts, and over pressure cracks, only after my brother got out and walked on ahead. The road was marked by Christmas trees shoved in holes every hundred feet or so. The sun made the glare of the ice and snow almost unbearable.

"This is like the prairies," I said.

"Except that you're over thirty feet of water," John said, watching for cracks. Out on the lake, only the occasional snowmobile and the odd colours of distant ice huts made with leftover lumber and paint gave us any indication we weren't on the moon, with its lunar drifts and snow craters. Closer to shore, the van picked up speed and we pulled up in front of an A-frame on the island's leeshore.

Inside, there was an airtight stove in one corner and a ceiling-to-floor window facing the lake. A dreamcatcher dangled from a long leather thong in the window. I knew instantly why my brother came here. Just like the lean-tos we used to have down at the river, when we were kids, this was his hideout. John split wood while my brother stoked the stove and soon it was crackling with dry birch. It always amazed me how my brother got people doing things for him. He was the firstborn. Our grandparents took him everywhere. Spoiled him, my father claims. By the time they got around to me, I was too independent. Sometimes, I think the genes got mixed up in our family. My girlfriend calls Adrian a she-man, and it's a compliment.

While they got the cabin ready, I explored the upper loft and deck which looked south across the lake. A handmade pine bed frame with a down comforter took up most of the loft. Above the bed was a shelf full of books on native lore, and one on sweatlodges lay on the bedside table. My brother had always looked more to Manitou than the stern Presbyterian God of our youth. A canoe was chained to the deck and a snowmobile parked in a nearby shed. A bluejay bounced out of the nannyberry bushes into a basswood tree behind the cabin. Piles of cleared brush stood in front of dozens of loose and knotty sumach — all things that the nurseries back home charged good money for waiting to be burned.

There wasn't much evidence of Lucia's hand here. My brother had decorated it: functional masculine rustic, complete with a cow skull we'd found out on Gladys Ridge and a horseshoe nailed over the back door. I liked it. I'd stopped camping out with my brother and his friends around the time I started growing breasts. I'm not sure they even noticed, I was such a tomboy.

John drove us out to one of the ice huts he owned. Huddled over the ice, with the propane heater going, we soon had our jackets and sweaters off and the door open. After baiting the drop lines, John salted the hole with minnows.

"What are we using?" Adrian asked.

"Three way spreader, gut wire."

John showed me as he baited the hooks. My brother is the fisherman in our family. Like golf, it seemed silly, but my brother was having fun. He and John were pulling in small perch, and I snagged a whitefish. All around us, we could hear the shifting of the ice and feel the pressure cracks ripping by and occasionally a sonic boom as the lake ice shifted.

"Don't worry," John said, "you're on two feet of ice." But it was eerie sitting in a hut out on a lake with a van parked outside.

We caught twenty perch and two whitefish, one of them mine and one John's. "An okay catch. Good thing we're not feeding our families," he ribbed me. As the sun started down, we went back to the cabin, where John cleaned the fish on the deck while my brother started peeling potatoes inside.

I brought John a beer, as he gutted each fish with a few swift cuts of the razor-sharp filleting knife.

"Thanks, I don't drink," he said, without taking his eyes off the knife, which skimmed under the fish bones, just ahead of his fingertips.

"I'll take it. You've got it open. I should have told you," my brother said, as he brought out a basin of water and went back in.

"It's okay. I quit — used to be a real scrapper, Suzy." John scooped the heads and guts into a bucket. "Got into a fight outside a bar on Queen Street. Guy pulled a knife. Right here," he looked up, using the fish knife to show me, "*Click*, it hits my rib. Stopped it. I'm standing there, can't believe it. He gets *real* mad. He does it again. *Click*. Hits my rib a second time. I run, bleeding like a pig, holding my side. Either there's a God, or I got lucky twice. I wasn't getting a third chance. Quit cold turkey right there. Not that I don't miss drinking, though." He smiled, his eyes serious.

My brother yelled from the cabin the fire was ready. I took the basin full of fish while John cleaned up. Adrian shook the filleted fish in a bag of flour and spice, and laid them in the butter bubbling in the cast iron grill.

On the counter, I saw a knife I hadn't seen in years. It was fawn-coloured, with *Sheffield* stamped on the blade, bone-handled with a small brass plaque. A.C. it said. My brother's initials.

"This the knife you used on that kid?" I asked, boldened by John's story and a couple of beers. I put it down in front of my brother's plate as we sat down to eat. "Where'd you *get* it?"

My brother flushed, "I was a wild man too, John. An eleven year old wild man. Mom kept it."

"You were *thirteen*. *I* was eleven."

"Anyway," he gave me a glance, over the oil lamp, "I was lucky, all considering. I had no intention of killing him. I *was* thirteen, whatever, I do remember it was my birthday three weeks before. I had no idea it could be so easy." He looked at the knife as he ate.

"The other kid was three years older, still in grade eight. Sat at the back of the class, lived in one of the rented houses by the C.P.R. shops. Probably had months to go before he could legally drop out. And hated our guts."

"And it was mutual," I said.

He looked at John. "My sister, a couple of friends and I were on our way to fish the irrigation canal behind the shops, our lunches tied to our belts and canteens full of Kool-Aid. I've told you about this, John."

He hadn't. John's eyes were intent on my brother's across the table.

"Our friend Kenny saw him first. Ledke was his name. He'd crossed the road." My brother's eyes were bright like Mom's when she told her Ontario stories.

"*Wade* Ledke, " I added.

"Whatever — I remember thinking 'We're dead meat. Run.' Every time we saw him, *we* crossed the street. And even when we did, he'd still cross back over and shove us around."

"And *I* said, 'We're not moving.' " I looked at my brother.

"I remember it was me, but you're probably right. You always had guts."

"So did he, John," I said. "Wait'll you hear what he did next."

"He killed him?" John laughed. "You two kill *me*."

"Anyway, I felt the knife in my pocket. This knife," he said, holding it. "My grandmother'd given it to me on my birthday — my granddad's, his name was Adrian Carp too. Someday, she'd said, I'd get his watch. I always wondered why she'd given me the knife then."

"More coffee?"

Adrian held up his cup. "I had to wait six more years for the watch."

"You're drif-ting. So *I* said, 'We're *not* moving!' " My brother shook his head between sips.

"So our friends Kenny and Tommy look at me. I'm no hulk. Suzy was taller than me then. One of them says, 'You guys nuts? He'll punch your lights out'."

"*I* was sick of running," I said.

"We were *all* sick of running. And my hand was on my knife. Suzy and I just stood there."

"Anyway, he comes at us like one of those clouds that hangs over the Stampede grounds in July. They dump, the river floods. Then they're gone, just like that. And you wonder if it was something you just thought up."

I looked at my brother. We used to have these imaginary friends when we were kids. His was Joe and mine was Betty. Everywhere we went it was Joe and Betty. Mom used to have to set a place for them at lunch.

"We were doomed . . . " John watched my brother as he spoke, then me. His eyes missed nothing. Adrian looked at me. "Our science teacher had talked about Cro-Magnon man in Science. His forehead, his walk. This guy was Cro-Magnon. You could see his eyes but not his chin tucked in. His eyebrows like one mean line drawn with a hair pencil."

"I thought he slowed down when he saw we weren't moving."

"The other two guys had dropped behind."

"He stopped two feet in front of us. First, he stared at Adrian. Then Kenny Dawes and Tommy Grogan. Then me. He sneered."

"Yeah, he says 'Where you *turds* going?' He dragged out turds like he enjoyed it."

"There was nowhere to go," I said.

"I didn't think, I just did it. I pulled out the knife and opened it. And as Ledke leaned towards us, I pointed the blade at his stomach." Adrian pointed the knife at the oil lamp, its smoky light making him look like the lead from Damien. "Ledke, you're dead."

"I don't remember you saying that . . . "

My brother gave me a nasty look. "Anyway, his eyes were clear and large and dark. I held the knife to his stomach. He'd sucked it in. The blade trembled against his shirt. My mouth went dry. I couldn't think of what else to say. My nerve was running out." Adrian took a long drink of coffee. "No, I didn't kill him. I *wanted* to."

"So did I." I looked at the knife in my brother's hand. "If Ledke had gotten me alone, it would have been an entirely different story."

"So he just took off. Booted it down an alley a block away." Adrian shrugged. "Kenny and Tom were impressed. Mom sure wasn't."

"Yeah, in fact, Kenny Dawes was so impressed, he told his mom about it. How my brother almost killed Wade Ledke. The neighbourhood was tough, but not that tough. Mrs. Dawes phoned my mom who spoke to my dad."

"Handed it over."

"We were both grounded for a hundred years . . . "

"At least . . . "

"Mom wanted Adrian to apologize to him. Fortunately, Dad was more understanding. I think he was proud, because he hid the knife in the dumbest place imaginable, behind the *good* glasses, over the kitchen sink. In our house, if you wanted someone to find something, that's where you hid it."

"I know. I visited my knife regularly. Fondly, opening and holding it before I hid it again."

"I'll never forget the look in his eyes. He was *scared*."

" 'Scared shitless,' Kenny said. But Ledke, scared? Of us? It was the knife. One thing, neither Kenny nor Tom pushed us around any more when we argued. But I wasn't sure if I liked this kind of respect." My brother looked at us and shook his head.

"You *loved* it. You just can't admit you did."

"Would you have done it?" John peered at my brother over the lamp.

"*I* would have," I said, "if I had this." I folded the knife shut.

"You'd've been one of my cases, if you had," John said.

"Don't know what I'd have done. Maybe if Suzy hadn't been there, I'd have run too. I think about it though. Life is good now. That could have changed it all."

"No doubt in *my* mind," I added.

"You're terrible. Next time, you're cleaning the fish," John pointed at me.

"There's no Ledkes among the kids I teach. Not visibly, anyway. The trouble-makers were streamed out long ago. But when we talk about the death penalty, all of these kids want it returned. One of them, the other day, nice enough kid, named Todd, thinks we should bring back capital punishment for *shoplifting*. A first-year business student, he tells me it's cheaper in the long run. The others all agree with him."

"He's got a point." I smiled at John.

"You've been reading too much *Alberta Report*." My brother looked over his glasses.

"They've had all the advantages," John added. "You ever tell them about Ledke?"

"John, I'd be up in front of a review committee so fast . . . "

"Really?" I asked.

"Really. Sure, sometimes I argue. How it's not the rage of the brute, but our fear of them that endangers us. I hate to think what *they* would have done." My brother reached into his pocket.

"Run, probably," John snorted.

I kept quiet.

"I still carry a knife. A gentleman's knife, the guy at Birk's called it. For opening letters, paring fingernails, that's all." He laid a small silver knife beside the bone-handled one. "I just carry it, I guess. Sometimes I'm afraid as I listen to my students talk. For the guys like Ledke."

"Bedtime cowboys," I gathered up the dishes. "You've got to get me back to the city first thing."

Before John left, he shook my hand. "See you next time, *killer.*" He laughed at Adrian.

"Great," my brother said, "I see a new nickname coming. Night John."

He put his arm around me and we stood on the deck, in our jackets, watching the lights of John's van bump around the island to his cabin. Bright bands of aurora borealis rippled across the clear sky on the other side of the lake. The hard sweet smoke of maple mixed with the snowy air. Over the horizon, the glow of the next town south was barely visible.

"Dad wants to know if you're *ever* coming home? I think I know, but what do you want me to tell him." I turned to face him.

"In Lucia's family, they say, 'Go home to bury the dead' —don't look back. Time is a great healer for some. Distance, for others."

"*You*, Adrian?"

"Tell him, yes. That's all you can do." He turned and went inside.

I watched him from the loft, taking down the sofa bed in front of the airtight. As he bent towards the stove, there was a stoop to his back I hadn't noticed.

Long after I went to bed, my brother waited by the fire stoking it. I could hear the stove door open and close, until I drifted into sleep, walking our old street, with Betty and my brother and Joe, without fear, without rage.

Hard Labour

Near the end of this southern Ontario day, there was no obvious sun in the sky, no real clouds, just a haze overhead stretching from Lake Ontario to the green bump of the Niagara Escarpment, so low and close, it wrapped around me like a hot wet towel. Heat waves shimmered off the highway as I drove back from the city. In the field I could see my father-in-law with his blue Ford tractor cap shading the top of his face as he drove the disc-harrow, trailing a small cloud of dust and birds who swept in to pluck up the exposed worms. The effect of shade made his red face look always angry. At the sight of my truck, Harold waved, raised the harrow and turned towards the farmyard.

    I pulled the truck around the fruit stand and into the coolness of the barn which doubled as a garage and fruit-packing shed. Closing the door behind me, I took my lunchpail and walked towards the house. My mother-in-law, Vivian, stood in the kitchen window, with only the part in her hair and the slope of her shoulders visible as she leaned over the kitchen sink. She looked up at the sound of the barn door closing and her face took a slight break from the grim heat of the kitchen, not to smile but to acknowledge my arrival and the end of the worst part of the day. My wife, Deb, coming in from the orchard caught me as I climbed the stairs into the house. Deb was breathless, excited as if something might be wrong.

"Hogs . . . " she blurted, "We're getting hogs."

"Hogs?" I said, "What do you mean, hogs?"

She looked in the direction of the fields and Harold.

"Don't let on you know, he's all excited," she continued. "It's supposed to be a surprise. He's giving us some hogs."

"Giving us? Deb, I'm excited too. What the hell do we want with hogs?"

"Never mind, we'll talk later, c'mon in the house. Here's Dad coming now."

"He got a deal, right?"

"You. C'mon supper's ready."

That's all we needed. Hogs. Another one of her dad's ideas. Another money-making, labour-intensive project for all of us to get involved in. Only to find out that for one reason or another, it won't work. Like the strawberry picker he invented. Using sheets of plywood and a system of braces and crossbars welded onto an old lowboy farm wagon, so that four strawberry pickers could lie down on it. I have to admit I liked that part as much as he did. Lying down on the job. Thing was, he would drive the tractor, naturally, which pulled the rest of us along, and we would pick. But in strawberry season you can count on rain almost every night and sometimes during the day. So the whole thing got bogged down, literally.

And then there were the geese. They were supposed to pick the weeds out of the strawberry patch. Worked fine until the geese ran out of weeds to eat. Then they started in on the strawberries and when the kids we hired to pick showed up in the morning, the geese wouldn't let them in the field. Even the dog wouldn't go near them.

Hogs. I didn't know anything about hogs, but one thing for sure — they meant work. More work. Pens to build, and troughs. They had to be fed. And there was probably some reason why you had to get up at four in the morning.

It sounded like part of Harold's general scheme to keep us on the farm. It was backfiring, though. Being a city boy, all I could think of was the work. Bad enough working in the dump all day driving a Cat, without having to come home to more work. Anyway, Deb and I were supposed to move into town come fall, as soon as we had the down payment for a house, which is why we were living with her parents. And last year's strike meant it was taking us longer than we expected.

Harold was against the idea, seeing two able, though unwilling farmhands disappearing. Besides, he reasoned, we could live in the old house when the new one was built at the end of the orchard. Sure. That meant we could get up and take care of customers who showed up late at night or early in the morning. I saw that one coming. Now at least I got to go into town to work during the day.

Sometimes, with the heat and the humidity, I wished I'd never let Deb talk me into leaving Alberta. At home when it was hot, it was dry. You never sweated. Here I was hauling irrigation pipe around after dark, knee-deep in wet clay, with Harold on the other end of the pipe, walking too fast. Or hoeing tomatoes on Saturday mornings. Thinking of Kenny and the guys breezing up north out of Calgary on Crowchild Trail, and then west down the long Cochrane hill, out towards the mountains past

Water Valley or Fallen Timber, with the boat on top of the van, and those trout that felt so good and heavy on the line.

Here, big dopey horseflies and invisible bugs that bit you in the night. When you woke up in the morning you were covered with red bumps. No thanks. And now hogs. No time off, no holidays. No more visions of Storybook Farms, the red painted barn with a weathervane, a white rail fence and a palomino pony in the corral.

I sat down at my usual place at the corner of the table next to his chair. There were only two places set with highball glasses and between them a bottle, without any label, full of homemade red wine. Neither Deb nor her mother ever set themselves a glass and were content to reach across my plate or Harold's for a drink. Whenever I offered to get them their own they refused.

The screen door banged, marking his arrival. It set in motion the flies that hovered around in the back porch and those that flew off the panes of the kitchen window. Splashing water punctuated the silence of the table as he washed his hands. He entered the kitchen, as he always did, and put his cap on top of the radio, which he turned to the agricultural report on the Buffalo station. He picked up the fly swatter from its nail near the fridge over top of the Rittenhouse Farm Equipment calendar with the picture of the calico kittens peering out of a basket. All without speaking a word. He put the fly swatter down beside his fork and poured himself a glass of wine. Harold's face was flushed with sun, his neck and cheeks red like a mask, his eyelids shaded white.

"Peas," he said.

Viv passed them, replying, "Potatoes?"

The casserole of noodles looked like tiny automobile radiator hoses covered with white cheese, disturbed by the odd dark meatball. It glistened on top and was crusty and burned around the edges. He helped himself with a big serving spoon, banging it down with a weighty splat on his plate.

"Bread?" he murmured, in no particular direction. Viv got up, shooting him a glance; still she got him his bread. As if there wasn't enough starch.

It had been 90 degrees that day, and the humidex, a summer equivalent of the chill factor, had been announced on the radio as being equal to 105 above. I looked at the food on my plate, and I sweated. A hot meal on a hot day. A fly strayed over the macaroni, the way gulls hover over the dump, flying reconnaissance for the others in the back porch. Harold reached for his fly swatter and crouched in wait. As the fly foolishly retreated to what it thought was a safe place on the lampshade above the table, Harold made his move. He dropped it within an inch of the casserole.

Whether it was the heat or everything else that day, Viv snapped.

"For chrissakes, leave the damned flies alone and eat your supper!"

He had his kill. In grim, good humour he put the fly swatter back and continued his supper. The announcer was reading the livestock report. At the mention of hogs, Harold spoke up, between mouthfuls.

"Need hand, after supper. Go into town. Get some lumber." Each phrase was interrupted by swallows. He had enough lumber stockpiled in the barn for anything he needed. Even said himself that he didn't like to buy lumber in the summer when the prices were high.

"Lumber?" I asked blankly.

Under the table I could feel Deb's heel hard on my toes.

Viv didn't say anything but got up from the table in her usual brisk fashion, moving about the kitchen, like a squirrel in an apron, stacking dishes nervously and scurrying about with a guilty sense of purpose. Harold wasn't letting on and I knew that Viv had already been over the details with Deb. And I knew that Viv didn't know that I knew and was waiting for Harold to tell me so she could be relieved of her conspiratorial guilt. And I wasn't about to make it any easier for him, not this time. Harold, I thought, this time I'm going along with you just to see how far this thing goes. Viv busied herself at the counter with the electric beater going. Deb cleared off the rest of the dishes while I reached for the last of the salad, the only cold thing left on the table. Harold sat there with his hand under his chin, his head cocked to one side pretending to listen to the radio, and I know he was trying to think up a way to bring in the hog idea gently. He knew me well enough to know I didn't like surprises, especially ones that involved me doing the work. Hang in there Harold, I thought, just like that fly. You're in this on your own.

Viv put a bowl of Devonshire cream and another of strawberries on the table. Deb brought four cut-glass dessert dishes and several teaspoons and three coffee cups. In the heat I never drank coffee after ten in the morning. At home I used to like to fill a glass up to the brim with ice and add a little ginger ale and rye which I'd strain through my teeth. So cold your fillings felt as if they'd shatter. The strawberries floated in a slippery red puddle of their own juice. The cream dully reflected the overhead light at me. My stomach felt like a wet bath towel being pulled through a wringer. I fished the strawberries out of my bowl, at least they were cold. When the cream came round, I choked back a gag and passed it to Viv who spooned great glops into her mouth. I tried not to look.

Passing on seconds, I took my own dishes to the sink. This was a bone of contention with me. How come Harold had these women serving him and I had to take my own dishes to the sink? I didn't mind doing it, I mean, but if he had offered for once to do the dishes or something, they'd both be falling all over themselves to do it for him, and when they said he didn't have to, he wouldn't. If I offered they would say yes without thinking. Talk about double standards.

"You wanna take the truck out of the shed?" he said, almost as if it were one word.

"Sure," I replied, not saying anything else.

The only truck we kept in the equipment shed was the old flatbed Dodge three ton that we used in apple season to haul apple boxes to the shipper in town. I was beginning to get worried. That old Dodge would carry a lot of lumber. I pulled my CAT hat down over my worried looks and headed out the back door. When I first started driving heavy equipment I thought these kinds of hats were for goofs. But sometimes they come in handy. Here I am. In redneck country with the king of rednecks himself. He actually watches the reruns of Archie Bunker seriously. Thinks Archie's his kinda guy. A guy who speaks his mind just like yours truly. And now I notice some of the students we hire for the summer looking at me the way I looked at the old guys when I first started working.

The Dodge misfired a couple of times and dust belched out of the stack, before it caught while I held down the starter pedal. I backed out gingerly with about an inch clear on each side. The doors on the shed were wagon-width, long before the days of Dodge flatbeds with West Coast mirrors. In the rearview, I could see Harold loping down the stairs towards the truck, putting on his hat with both hands, pulling it down close to his ears, farmer style.

Kenny always used to say you could tell a man's job by the way he wore his hat. Farmers pull them down to ear level with the brim just above the eyebrows and pointed straight ahead. Cat operators wear 'em high up and off the forehead with a Mickey Mantle crease folded carefully in the brim. Had to be a regulation CAT diesel hat too, not your Taiwan imitation bought at Canadian Tire by some suburban accountant who has trouble keeping his Winnebago between the lines on holiday weekends. The truckers never had the mandatory three greasy finger prints on the brim that the operator had. But the sunglasses gave them away. With all those beaners keeping your pupils cranked open full bore, a 40 watt light bulb, never mind unadulterated sunlight, can be pretty hard on the old eyes.

Harold climbed in without a word. The old Dodge fussed and farted a few times before lurching into gear as I double-clutched my way up from first to fourth. If only Kenny could see me now. Joe Farmer goes to town. Easy Rider rifle rack in the back window and Harold Chamber Farms, Grimsby, hand painted on the doors. He'd die laughing. Harold, as usual, didn't have much to say, and the Dodge didn't have a radio. Whenever I edged up closer to the speed limit he'd look over. Harold didn't believe, as most farmers don't, in doing the speed limit. He also didn't believe in radios in work vehicles. Too hard to do thirty-five miles an hour on the Queen E., watch the scenery, take up the whole road, chew gum and have to listen to a radio on top of all that.

Ever since I got here and found that the tree in the front yard with the dirty looking blossoms was a magnolia, I keep thinking that southern Ontario is the deep south of this country. The more time I spend on the farm the more I believe it. The other day the O.P.P. raided a Klan meeting in a town just north of here. I knew Harold was wondering why I wasn't talking. I'm not known for my quietness. Stew, Harold, stew, I thought.

The lumber yard was outside town on the end of the strip of implement dealers, tire stores, donut shops, and hamburger stands. They had the order stacked and loaded on a forklift, waiting for us. The kid on the order desk was missing two important teeth at the side of his mouth and looked like he'd been trying to grow a moustache for the last three of his eighteen years. His blue uniform shirt had the name Roy stitched in red lettering over the pencil pocket. As he wrote up the order he kept shaking his hair out of his eyes like he had some kind of nervous tic. He had a homemade tattoo on his arm. It was a crude heart with the name Sherry with an arrow through it. Harold, funny man he is, said: "How you doin' Roy?" To me it sounded suspiciously like Boy. The look the kid gave us let us know he'd heard this a hundred times before and the only reason he was wearing this dumb shirt with his name on it and not a Guns 'N Roses T-shirt was because his boss made him.

Harold followed him out to the yard and I pulled the truck alongside the forklift, and as the kid lowered the load onto the deck the truck shuddered under the weight. By the number of four-by-fours it was easy to see that Harold had more in mind than building apple crates. The dump was bad enough. With the flies, the garbage, the gulls, and the gullshit all over the cab of the packer. Then to come home to more of the same. I started to boil at the thought of unloading all that lumber in the dark. By the time we got back it would be pitch black and with that load of four-by-fours hanging over the back of the truck we wouldn't be able to put the Dodge in the shed overnight. Harold paid Roy and got back in the truck. At least we didn't have to load it. I tensed my hands on the steering wheel like I was trying to strangle it and eased the clutch out. Harold must have sensed something was wrong and that maybe, just maybe, word of his plan had gotten out. The communication link between Deb and her mother could either make or break whichever of Harold's schemes didn't stand up on their own, and that was most of them. Wives are like mothers when it comes to reading minds and Deb always said I couldn't keep a secret if I wanted to. Like there was a video screen built into my forehead that betrayed what the lower half of my face was trying not to say. Well Harold read it somehow, for on the way back out of town he pointed and grunted in his usual eloquent way to Tim Horton's.

The last thing I wanted right now was a dry chocolate donut that dropped coconut like dandruff and a hot cup of coffee when I could feel the sweat circle under my shirt inching closer to my belt. It was a bribe, I saw that for what it was. But it stalled the job of unloading.

"Sure," I said, making my first dent in the silence. Harold usually counted on my banter to fill in for the lack of a radio. He'd contribute the odd grunt and occasionally came up with some anecdote which came out more like a riddle which left me to puzzle over what he meant and him to figure out what I had been saying that had made him bring it up in the first place. I ground the shift down into second without double clutching to make a point. Harold was always impressed by the fact that for a city boy I could double clutch. At the painful rattle from the gear box he looked over the way he did when I got too close to the speed limit, and his lips looked like a three-inch-wide mark made with a chalk and ruler. He would get mad at me for not asking him what he wasn't telling me that I already knew. No. Couldn't be his fault no how.

He took up his position at the corner of the counter. That meant he didn't have to look me in the eye because the only place I could sit was on the corner right angle to him or beside him, both seats being empty. Either way suited his offhand way of dealing with things, including conversation. I sat down beside him. He had himself in a corner literally, that he couldn't get out of, and he didn't have Viv or Deb to bail him out and I wasn't being of much use. I pulled my hat down low over my face to cover the video screen that showed a detonator wire running to a box labelled TNT. It wasn't the first time I'd felt this way. But I kept my mouth shut and the lower half of my face immobile except for washing down the dry donut with coffee. I could never understand in a place as humid as this, where anything that stands still starts to rot, how donuts could go stale. I knew he wanted me to break the impasse by asking casual-like what the lumber was for. Even I knew he was thinking that you don't build apple boxes with four by fours. I said nothing. He said nothing. The waitress smiled my way as we left and the top of my hat glowered at her.

After the silent drive home I pulled the truck around the back of the old barn at the end of the orchard as he directed. For the first time I saw that he had levelled off the area with the scarifier on the tractor. Now I knew he was really worried about me finding out. As the resident equipment operator he usually got me to do the grading and the ploughing. Still I played dumb, hiding for all it was worth behind my greenhorn city slicker routine, and pulled my hat down further. By this time both of us were fuming. He was out of the truck even before it stopped and was waving me back. Which made little sense. It was pretty obvious where to go. Even in the dark you had two acres to back up in without hitting anything. Besides, the backup lights were strictly ornamental and all he was doing was giving me something to run over. And if ever I was tempted.

It began with the boards. I'd reach for three on my end and Harold would reach for four on his, the same way we hauled irrigation pipe. Still, at sixty he was in better shape than I'd ever been at twenty.

Maybe if it was my farm then I could have gotten more enthusiastic about unloading lumber in the back field at ten at night. I swore under my breath and he grabbed even more lumber in his own fury. As he pulled it off the truck I shoved for all it was worth, imagining that I was forcing it down his throat. He was probably thinking of each board as being me and what a nice job the chain saw would do. I couldn't stand it any longer.

"Harold, slow down, for godsakes," I said, the godsakes being admittedly less loud than the slow down.

"Look," he said, "if you don't want to do it, just say and I'll do it by myself."

I recognized the guilt strategy. Deb had taught me everything her family knew about guilt.

"I didn't say I didn't want to do it, I said slow down!"

By this time he was pulling the boards off without me and I was shoving them off any way they'd go. The pile of wood at the end of the truck was no longer orderly and the stench of exhaust hung in the sticky dark air.

"If you don't want to help, just go in the house!" he said. That was a low blow. He meant, in the house with the women. From the man who adored Archie Bunker.

"Listen Harold, I hate stacking lumber in the dark and I hate hauling irrigation pipe, but I'm doing it aren't I? I don't have to like something to do it so why don't you pay attention to someone besides yourself."

I was now in up to my neck. I heard footsteps. The dog had come down from the house wagging, barking and giving me his dumb Rin Tin Tin to the rescue look.

"Your problem is you want everything handed to you. Your generation. Afraid of work."

I knew he was misquoting his American idol and I'd heard all this before when he waxed poetic after a few glasses of Aaron Schier's still liquor. But he was on the defensive. He hadn't brought up the hogs yet and I knew he wasn't leading up to it.

"Who are you trying to fool?" I said, putting both boots in my mouth at once. "You're the one who wants something for nothing."

Without pausing in his work he said, "Huh?" Angrily, both of us worked faster than ever.

"What about hogs, Harold? How much you know about raising hogs, Harold?" Hitting in his wallet and his pride at once.

"You stay out of this!" he sputtered. "Me and Mom just manage fine without you or Deb. We have 'til now, and will later."

He was going for the heartstrings now. Me and her against him and Viv.

"Harold, we told you when we moved out here we'd stay just long enough to find a house in town. Now you're buying hogs and dreaming up more work than ever. It's crazy. You're sixty years old, Harold, and Viv is going like a workhorse."

I knew then where I had heard this argument before. My old man. Wanting me to help him start a contracting business. Always an angle on how to make a fast buck. Dreaming of a shortcut to easy street. Last thing in the world I wanted to run was a two-man contracting business. I hated working indoors and the kind of people you meet didn't thrill me. But I didn't like working outside enough to become a dirt farmer in southern Ontario. And have to shovel pig shit at that. The dump was bad but it was a forty-hour week and you didn't take your work home with you. But I felt bad. I knew this would get us nowhere.

"Look, Harold, I think we better settle this in the house."

By this time the dog was barking hard at me. Reckoning that since I was the newest arrival it must be my fault. Trust a dog to be that loyal and dumb.

"Just go to hell. Forget it. We'll do just fine, just bloody fine."

I knew he was really mad. He almost never swore. I felt like a real jerk.

"What's goin' on out here, Harold? Why are you doing this after dark?" It was Viv, taking charge as she always did, but only after everything completely fell apart. She started to help him and curse him between each board.

"You could have waited 'til morning. Harold, that lumber isn't going to walk away godammit!" she said, her voice rising to an irritating pitch each time she said his name.

I felt sorry I'd ever said anything and wished I was one of those boards he was slamming down on the pile. Together the three of us finished unloading. Viv shot me one of her famous head-levelling glances, and when I took the truck back up to the yard I could see Deb waiting in the kitchen window with her arms folded across her chest. What could I have done? I kind of half agreed with the old bugger. I just didn't want to get roped into something I didn't want. Not that my choice was any great shakes either. Can't blame a guy for tryin', the old man used to say.

My hands were shaking so much I had trouble getting the truck back in the shed and scraped one of the mirrors going in. I'd never hear the last of that. I heard the screen door bang and saw by the upstairs light that Harold had gone right to bed. When I got into the kitchen Viv gave me one of her 'well what have you got to say for yourself?' looks.

"Viv," I said, "we're moving." Opening my first line of real communication since we'd been here. Deb looked a little surprised.

"We've been looking at houses and I think we're going to take the first one that seems reasonable. We'll come out on the weekends and Deb can drive me to work and come out in the truck if she wants, but I'm not going along with this any longer."

"Have it your way," she said. "We wanted to help you kids out."

I felt like a shit. I couldn't tell if she was mad or if she was going to cry. I knew she was saving face, more for Harold's sake than her own. Deb was caught in the middle and when I went upstairs it was a long time before she finally came up to bed. When she did I felt a tentative arm over my waist, as if she were equally bewildered by a choice neither of us wanted to make.

When I got home from work the next day I could see the tractor hadn't been out of the shed. Deb met me in the yard and said that Viv had taken Harold in to the doctor's. He'd been complaining of chest pains and he'd always had high blood pressure on and off. We ate alone that night, and in silence. After supper I went out to the barn. On his workbench I found the rough drawing of the plans for the hog pen. I got the posthole auger and a tape and went out to where we unloaded the lumber. The auger barely scraped the hard clay. With all my weight pressed into the handle I turned it, walking around the shallow hole as it went slowly deeper.

My old man. Always on the lookout for a deal. Like the time he paid some construction boss twenty bucks and a case of beer for a truckload of scrap lumber. In his greed he forgot to check one thing. Every one of the boards in the load had six-inch rusty spikes every foot or so. The old man paid me five bucks and said he'd give me five more when I finished. That weekend I took his crowbar, a hammer and my twelve year old frame out to the shop at the back. After twenty minutes of grunting and the bar slipping out of my hands I sat down on the lumber and started to cry. I needed the five bucks to go to camp. I didn't want to give it back. And yet I couldn't do what the old man wanted.

In the end he did the work himself while I looked on. He let me keep the five bucks, but it wasn't the same.

I heard the car pull into the driveway up the lane. I didn't look up but kept digging. The hardwood handle of the auger scraped skin off my palms. Slowly the hole got deeper, then finally deep enough to hold the four-by-four posts leaning cockeyed and unsupported. One by one they went in, forming the outline of the hog pen. A little after the sun went down Deb came out bringing the thermos and two cups. In the cool of sunset we sat on the woodpile.

"He'll be all right," she said. "The doctor told him he'll have to watch it. His blood pressure is high again."

"That's all?"

"So Mom says."

"Think he'll slow down?"

"He won't. He never has. The farm's everything," she said, with more than a trace of bitterness. "By the way, that realtor I called phoned back today. She's got a couple of places for us to look at."

The tone of her voice told me this decision was mine.

"Tomorrow, after work?" I asked.

She nodded.

"What about the farm work though? How are we going to keep up, Deb?"

"The worst of the season is by, most of the summer crops are in and if you do the ploughing he'll be all right on his own. The apples Mom and I can handle with the pickers. And you'll be home in time to help pack. Anyway, the doctor just said for him to rest for a few days and gave him a prescription. That's what Dad told Mom he said."

"He's bought the hogs already, hasn't he?" I asked.

"Two weeks ago."

"I'll finish the pen. Since he's already bought them." When we got back to the house I saw his prescription on the counter beside the sink. Nitro glycerin, it said. He had more than high blood pressure.

I finished off the rest of the pen after work. When we weren't in town looking at houses. Aaron Schier came over to visit and bring Harold a bottle of his best potato champagne. He saw me working and when he came over he rolled his eyes at the sight of the pen.

"It's all he needs," Aaron said.

"Tell me about it," I replied. "Want to hand me those spikes?" Aaron helped me out for the rest of the week while Harold rested. When he got back he stayed clear of me. And the ploughing was done by the time I got home. Slowly, the hogs were becoming my project, like it or not. He'd bought them from Eddie Rittenhouse whose brother owned the equipment dealership, and between the rest of the Rittenhouse brothers they'd most of the things worth owning in the entire county, including the winery and the cannery.

They were delivered early one morning after I'd gone to work. When I got home that night there they were with their blunt noses, no-name faces, all five of them in the new pen. They were more grey than pink. And they were big, each one dwarfing the dog by a couple of hundred pounds. The huge bodies moved as one mass around the pen. Surprisingly, they weren't all that dirty. Aaron told me they were supposed to be a hell of a lot smarter than your average horse. Well, their heads were big enough. At least some of it had to be brain. But I hated watching them eat, the way they mashed their faces into the slop. In minutes it was gone.

We found a house in an old neighbourhood on the edge of downtown, overlooking the canal. It was kind of small, but it was all brick with a carport and central air conditioning, which sold me right away. There was a lot of work to be done, painting, retiling, and insulating, but the price was right. Deb and I agreed to spend nights working on it so we could move right in after the apples were off the trees. She had a winter job lined up at a hardware store a few blocks away. Harold didn't say a word. He kept out of my way and I kept out of his. Viv, on the other hand, while she was a little miffed about us moving, came in to help us strip the floors, and she was as excited as if it were her own.

Then one drizzly Sunday in October, Viv came by for a few hours and ended up staying for supper. It was getting dark as she left ahead of us in the car. I said we'd follow in a few minutes. All the way back to the farm, Deb and I rattled on about how we'd throw a party for everybody, including some of her old school friends, once we got the place finished.

When I drove into the farmyard all the lights were on in the house and the back door was banging wide open on its hinges. As we pulled into the drive, the truck headlights lit up the lane behind the barn leading to the hog pen. I could hear the dog barking furiously and in the headlights saw the outline of Viv running towards the pen with a rifle. Deb jumped out of the truck and said:

"Go see what's going on, I'll call Aaron."

As I drove up to the pen I could see Viv firing blindly into the hogs. The dog howled and snapped at them through the fence rails, throwing his whole weight against the gate. I slammed on the brakes just in front of the pen. Viv paid no attention. She was already hysterical and when the gun stopped firing she threw it at one of the hogs.

Then I saw why she was shooting. His hat lay trampled and muddied a few feet away from the trough. Beside it was the slop pail, tipped on its side not far from his hand. He lay on the ground where he had fallen, twisted in pain, his other hand to his chest. Under the glare of the truck headlights and the yard light, I realized what the shadows didn't tell. He had been there for some time. His mouth was slightly ajar; the skin was gone from the soft parts of his nose, most of his face, his mouth, and gone were his ears. The bones of his fingers were exposed and jagged. I grabbed Viv back just as she started to open the gate. The dog shot in before I could close it. Behind me I could hear Deb yelling as she came running from the house.

I turned and shouted at her, "Stay there! Don't come any closer!"

By this time Viv had all her weight on my shoulder. Deb was crying as she took her mother who was now shaking and incoherent.

"Deb, take her to the house. Get a doctor, she's going into shock."

Maddened by the shots of the .22 and the dog lunging through them again and again like a rabid animal, they moved around the pen, their huge bodies pressing against each other until they cornered him between the trough and the fence rails. One of them kneeled on its front legs, bleeding from the shoulder, its front legs crippled by the .22. It got up, struggled, then toppled forward. The others were spattered with blood. Which she had shot and which had been missed, I couldn't tell. All of them had blood on them. I got the .303 out of the truck, found the clip in a box under the seat and slipped it into the rifle. The well-machined click of the shells into the firing chamber was the only thing I was sure of now. I rested the gun on the top rail of the fence. The first shot rammed into the chest of the largest one. His body tumbled backwards against the others. The explosion of the gun drowned their squealing and the baying of the dog. I put the rifle to my shoulder again, once, twice, three times, four. The recoil of the shots sent the butt pounding into my shoulder; it felt as if it had been smashed with a mallet. My ears rang, whirring with the sound of gunfire.

The dog sank his teeth into the leg of one of the hogs and whipped his head from side to side in a frenzy. Another jerked its hindquarters and feebly tried to rise. I lowered the sight and pulled the trigger one more time. Nothing. The clip was empty. I didn't hear the truck come up behind me until its lights filled the air. A hand encircled the stock of the gun. Aaron Schier. I could hear a siren and see flashing lights on the concession road. Another truck pulled into the yard. Alerted on the party line, other neighbours were arriving. I looked first at Aaron and then his hand on the gun. I held tight for a moment. He looked at me as if he wasn't sure. I released my hold and gave him the spare clip. He inserted it and fired into the last animal.

By now the dog was completely spooked, his fur filthy with blood and wet clay. He limped as he tore up and down the pen, his tongue hanging long and sideways out of his mouth. Together it was all we could do to catch him. He would not let us near the body of his master. We had no choice. As Aaron held him by the scruff of his neck to keep him from snapping, I pulled an old feed sack over the animal's head. The dog was livid with both fear and rage.

Neither the sack nor the nylon rope I'd tied around his feet would hold him long. I took his back legs and Aaron held him carefully by his muzzle and front feet. We laid him on the grass between the apple trees. Aaron turned me towards the house. I got as far as the truck and put my head down on the warm, wet hood. When I heard the shot and the soft moan of the dog, I did not look up. On my hands I could smell the blood. I lay there for what seemed a long, long time.

And when the ambulance arrived, I rose and walked slowly not to the pen, but towards the house, where every window was full of light, where my wife needed me now, knowing the silent and far greater need was my own.

Country Music Country

When Kenny Dawes died last Thursday he was a federal prisoner. He'd robbed the same 7 Eleven three times in four days. No mask, nothing. And he had a long prior record.

His sister Lori phoned the next day on Friday and asked me to call Adrian in Toronto. Kenny had died the day before, she said, and his body was being sent down from the penitentiary in Prince Albert. I told Adrian we'd go fishing afterwards up at Gran's place, since he'd be here anyway. The Highways Department gives me time off for all the winter weekends they call us in for snowstorms. And this was turning out to be the kind of funeral people came to only because they had to. I wondered if anyone besides us would actually come. The Kenny Dawes we knew died a long time ago.

Adrian arrived on the Monday morning flight. I got to the airport early to watch his plane come in. I'd taken that flight many times myself when Deb and I still lived out east. For some reason, it flew first over the city then doubled back from the south over our old neighbourhood. He'd be up there now over the irrigation canal which sprawled like a muddy snake alongside the weave of tracks and the huge yards and rail shops. The plane flew too high and too fast to see our old houses, but if he looked closely, he'd see the streets, 18th, 19th, 20th and so on, that ran out like postmarks from the small green stamp of park and to the west of it, over the brown hills beyond the new subdivisions where the explosives plant had been, the old river road crossed by a new expressway, and beyond all that, the blue ridges rising up to the sharp white peaks of the mountains seventy miles west. No matter how long I was away, it was home. Like coming into my parents' house to the first shock of all the smells that I'd always known, with all the fears and memories I half hoped I'd forgotten.

When his flight was announced, I waited with the others by the glass doors that led in from the arrivals ramp. Two guys in white Stetsons, one with a guitar and the other with a banjo, were setting up. Then a dark-haired woman in her white cowboy hat, the official symbol of the city, and a pink square dance skirt, walked up to the doors and put down a bucket with a long rod in it. I felt kind of stupid, but I had my boots and boot pants on too. During Stampede week you could feel dumb two ways, if you dressed Western or if you didn't.

Adrian thankfully was one of the first through the doors. Every time I see him now he's a little more grey and paunchy. The rest of us were getting pot bellies too. Just then the two guys broke into a bluegrass run and the woman took the rod and started branding people with the rubber stamp on the end of it. Adrian got one too. I sure wouldn't want to have *my* funeral during Stampede week.

"Hey Tom, howdy," he said quietly, but in the spirit of things.

"Yeah," I said, taking his hand and we hugged the way men do in crowds, firm but brief.

Driving the long road in from the airport, we bantered on about the drought this spring, the nurses' strike last winter, our settling-in talk we always did.

"What's that, over past CFCN hill?" Adrian pointed to a large white tower on the ridge of the highest point of land just west of the city that held the T.V. station and tower.

"High tech ski jump," I said. "You missed the party last year. Want a tour later?" I asked a little hesitantly.

"So I hear. It was a conscious decision," he said. "And thanks, but I'll pass. I'm trying to remember the way I left it." I knew he'd say that, but I understood, and I didn't want to admit I'd taken part in the celebrations at Olympic Square each night after the games.

"You know that whole block where the Billingsgate fishmarket was? It's gone — and the Queens too."

"There a law here against anything old?" he grumped at me, as I steered the truck towards downtown.

"My old man once helped tear down a house on Eighth Street and Seventh Avenue. They put up the Baptist Church with the tower that had four steel balls on it. He put a penny in each one and welded them shut. Twenty years later he's working on the Sandman Inn on the same spot."

We talked about everything except Kenny. We'd agreed to go right to the funeral home as the service was early in the afternoon.

Some things never change. The funeral home looked like a fake church. Here, if there's four corners, there's a gas station on one and churches on the other three. The terrible twins in this town: God and gasoline. This one on

17th Avenue near the Stampede grounds had white gravel in the flower beds and two plaster statues, a doe and her fawn, standing in a bed of red geraniums. One thing Adrian and I always agreed on was that there never was a shortage here of religious nuts or bad taste.

"Bambi," he said, as we got out of the truck.

"Venison," I returned. I had an image to keep up.

When I worked for the City out east, I knew a guy who worked in the cemetery who said there's big money in funerals. Three hundred bucks for a vault. That's the concrete box like a septic tank that goes around the coffin. He'd spray them with gold paint so the cemetery could charge another two hundred. And he heard from the fellow who drove the hearse that the coffins ranged from Cadillacs to Chevs or worse. They always show you the low-end Chev, then the Cadillac, before showing you the mid-range ones. Naturally no one wants to seem cheap so they buy the mid-range ones — the ones with the highest markup. I wasn't looking forward to this.

As we walked from the truck a woman in a sari with a white hat on went by towing two little boys in short pants, each with matching red straw cowboy hats with whistles they took turns blasting.

"Get a load of that," Adrian pointed across the street. "Only in Calgary."

Atop the garage was a billboard. "Shroud of Turin", it said. "July 3–12. On the Midway." They were everywhere, and I read in the paper that it was packing in the crowds, even though what the billboard didn't say was that it was only *pictures* of the Shroud of Turin. I was kind of embarrassed I hadn't noticed it first. You get so you take this stuff for granted here. "At The Calgary Exhibition and

Stampede. Home of the Greatest Outdoor Show on Earth!" the billboard also said.

"Don't worry, it'll be at the C.N.E. in August too," I warned him.

We always got into this. Adrian wanted me to move back. He'd argue East, I'd argue West, even though we both knew this old east-versus-us stuff was too dumb for words. I wasn't crazy about being back here, but it was home. You hate the place and you hate to leave. After Deb's dad died a couple of years ago, there wasn't much reason for her staying in Ontario. Her mom sold the farm and my parents were still here, so we moved back.

We walked across the parking lot and up the steps of the funeral home. Inside it was dark except for a fountain of trembling glass rods with different coloured lights rising out of the centre. The attendant showed us into the small chapel and gave us a short printed program.

For a guy who drove Kenworths and Macks, his coffin sure was a beater. Made of thin plywood, with cheap chrome handles like those on kitchen drawers, it had what looked like a denim-covered lid. Lori said on the phone that's what the government provided. Kenny was still federal property and she was afraid she'd need a court order to get him something else. And I don't really think his mom had all that much money. One thing for sure, Kenny didn't. I was surprised a cop wasn't there to make sure this wasn't his last scam.

We were only ten minutes early for the service but as the attendant led us to the front of the chapel, we could see just four people there. When we filed by the coffin, both of us stopped. I didn't want to look, but I did. My stomach jumped at what I saw.

His mouth was closed so you couldn't see his two missing front teeth. Not from a fight, but falling as he got off the bus one winter night. What was also missing were his shades and his Jack Daniels hat. Kenny always wore shades, day or night, and the dirty blue hat his cousin had brought him back from Arkansas because you can't buy them here.

He was so small and so old, at thirty-six. He looked like a little old man in his sweater, like the ones his mother used to order from the Sears catalogue. The kind that no one wore anymore, a white Irish cardigan with fake wooden buttons. His skin looked cold and pale as river ice. I couldn't bear it.

A long time ago we'd flipped through the catalogue before the junior high graduation. In our neighbourhood, they made a big deal of it then. It was years before I realized why. Not too many of us even made it through high school. So he got a green V-necked vest, forest green the catalogue said, and mine was striped of many colours like a calico cat. We waited for weeks, fearing that our sweaters wouldn't come. If they didn't, we said we wouldn't go. But they did and we went.

They'd be our armour we thought. Adrian went with his sister. Neither Kenny nor I had dates. So we sat out that dance with our expectations, our parents' and the school's for us, none of them coinciding. Not knowing then who we were, let alone who we were supposed to be. Our sweaters hung on us like cheap false skins. And that was how he looked now, a little old man in a toupé with someone else's skin. We're burying somebody, but it sure isn't Kenny Dawes, I thought, as Adrian took my arm. I'd been standing there too long.

But the truth is, Kenny was a drunk. Even Adrian had no patience with him when he drank, and over the last five years that was almost always. When he was around, he'd ramble on. We stopped listening to him. Funny though — other than that, he never acted drunk. The last time we all went fishing together, about four years ago, Adrian found an empty mickey under the truck that hadn't been there before lunch. Kenny didn't show it, though. And he always saved his really stupid stuff for when we weren't around. We calmed him down, I guess. But usually we heard about it later.

He pulled a couple of B & E's, kited a few cheques, and he stole a tow truck once. And probably there were others. But he always got caught. He had a big mouth and sometimes got in fights. Height and weight, like hindsight, were not his strong points. He always lost. But the 7 Eleven stunt was the dumbest. He was charged with two counts of robbery and one of armed robbery because he had something under his jacket. It turned out to be an O Henry bar he'd shoplifted before the robbery. But the clerk didn't know that. We all figured, even his sister, that he'd die a rubby. But not at thirty-six.

When the organist began to play, the Anglican minister, a guy I'd never seen before, stepped to the front. Kenny and I were Anglican. Adrian was United. Kenny had been a server at church and the minister used to have him ring the bell sometimes. Kenny used to ride the rope and when you went by the cloak room you'd see him going up and down, his feet lifting off the floor with each ring of the bell. Then one day he got into the communion wine. All he got was sick. It was only Welch's grape juice he admitted later. But the minister told him to go home and stay there until he smartened up. Kenny stayed home.

We all stood as the minister read from the Book of Common Prayer. He was broad and solid with a large voice that didn't need a microphone. As he talked his Adam's apple floated up and down like a fish bobber. He knew Mrs. Dawes, but he talked about Kenny in the vague way ministers do when they don't really know someone. I wasn't paying attention and watched the window off to the side beyond the coffin where the family was. The window was darkened and the lights were low. It was a short service and there was no eulogy, just a reading of the 23rd Psalm. That had to be Mrs. Dawes' idea. She was the churchgoer in their house. As we filed out, the organist played "Amazing Grace". I tried to think what was amazing right now about Kenny.

The last religious experience we had was when we snuck into the Stampede grounds by wading to our waists through the Elbow River, wandering with dripping pants, and eating corndogs, to watch the Alligator Girl from Florida who turned out to be one very overweight old girl with a skin disease. Kenny weaseled his way backstage and into her trailer to get her autograph. He got all freaked out because she tried to kiss him, so he said.

Adrian had his arms crossed tightly and was blinking a lot and I froze my face, both of us trying not to cry. His funeral, like his life, was short. The program the attendant gave us said that he'd be cremated privately. At least we didn't have to go to the cemetery.

Afterwards, Mrs. Dawes came out of the windowed section to thank the minister, and Lori invited us back to her mother's place. I left Adrian to talk to her while I got the truck.

The sunlight was garish after the funeral home. Traffic was backed up waiting to go into the parking lot of the fairgrounds and crowds of happy people made their way along the sidewalk, most in cowboy hats and shorts, some with cameras.

That was that. I wished. Adrian was more like that. He'd usually explode and a hour later forget about it. Me, it just worms around inside for a long time, getting fainter and smaller until one day I don't even realize it's gone. Then it's okay. It was like that after Deb's dad died too.

I got the truck and pulled around the front. Adrian seemed to be taking his good time. When he finally did come out, his eyes were red and puffy. We drove from 17th Avenue up to 12th, bypassing the long line of cars going towards the fairgrounds. Mrs. Dawes still lived in the same small house in the old neighbourhood.

"Aroma Avenue," Adrian remembered, as we crossed the bridge onto the old road up over Scotsman's Hill with its grand and free view where we'd used to watch the fireworks bursting over the fairgrounds every night during the Stampede.

"Would we go any other way?" I said.

The old road was still the shortest way home. For years it was the only way. And as we passed the long line of red and blue horse trailers and the painted railway cars of Conklin Shows parked along the river behind the fairgrounds, and then drove past the Shamrock Hotel and by the poultry plant and cut through the stockyards, it was obvious why we called it Aroma Avenue. Every day on the bus home from school, and later work, even with our eyes shut we knew exactly where we were — by our noses. First the chicken pluckers got on in their slippery gumboots, smelling like raw chicken. No fate worse than that we thought. Even the railyards were preferable to the Pinecrest poultry plant where no one really admitted to working, the kind of job you took between jobs. And then halfway home there was the brewery, then the distillery, then the rendering plant with its burnt hair and hide smell, and finally, the last turn, the deadman's curve onto the bridge, where the boozy smell of crude blew off the oil refinery on the home stretch past the railway shops.

When we crossed over the new bridge, the old one stacked neatly beside on the bank for sale, apparently government surplus, Adrian finally spoke. He wasn't usually this quiet. Since moving there he'd become more like those frantic people I once met in Toronto who were so busy they couldn't stand to let you finish a sentence.

"Would you mind if we left later tomorrow?" And I knew Adrian well enough to know he was leading into something.

"I said I'd ask you first," he said.

"Told who you'd ask what?" I stared at him.

"There's the cremation," he started.

"Oh no," I turned to him. "You go if you want, but there's no way. Enough's enough."

But Adrian seemed offended.

"That's not what I meant. I wanted to ask you first."

I could feel him looking at me. I concentrated on the road.

"I was thinking," he said quietly, "we could offer to take Kenny's ashes up north with us. Lori said he always raved about our trips up there."

Sometimes Adrian had the damnedest ideas, like when he was into his hippie thing, saying he thought we should all share everything. Meaning girlfriends, money. Neither of which he had. And everything also had to be all natural. This sounded like one of those ideas.

"Well?" He was waiting. And we were running out of time. Mrs. Dawes' place was only ten blocks away.

I knew he had already offered. Mrs. Dawes didn't have any money. We were old friends of Kenny and his current pals, whoever they were, sure weren't stepping forward. But one thing worried me.

"Not in the cab. Jesus Christ, Adrian."

"Calm down, it's only his ashes."

But I'd already been suckered. We had only four more blocks.

"You shit." I glared at him. He didn't say anything.

"But you dump him. Then we go fishing. This is too weird."

Adrian seemed slightly more cheerful. And I'd thought we'd gotten rid of Kenny.

I dropped Adrian off in front of the Dawes' tiny bungalow and parked. When I got there, Mrs. Dawes greeted me.

"Tommy," she said, using my childhood name in the warm fuzzy way that never failed to soften me, as she'd always done. She took my hands. I was half glad now we were taking Kenny. She seemed not sad but relieved, maybe because people had shown up.

Ivy Dawes is what my mother calls a survivor. First her husband, and now Kenny. The old man had left her for a new model he'd been trying out at the office. Kenny had never forgiven him. His father was the timekeeper at the Shops, but he carried a lunchpail, they all did. And he was the shortest little guy with a big temper. Like the time he'd spent all this money on hockey equipment for Kenny one Christmas, all blue in the colours of the Toronto Maple Leafs. Then he found out that Kenny wasn't going to the rink but to my house. Neither of us had made the team because we couldn't skate backward. We'd play Monopoly and then Kenny would put his hockey sweater on and go home. So it wasn't exactly a surprise the old man wasn't at the funeral home.

I mumbled my regrets to Mrs. Dawes and gave her an embarrassed half hug and then made my way towards the kitchen doorway. It was a while, a long while, since I'd been out to visit either her or Kenny. Adrian was talking to Lori, and her husband Robert was pouring drinks in the kitchen. Lori was a cashier now at the Co-op and Robert managed the Shell station on the South hill. Their two kids, Shauna and Robbie, were sitting bored on the chesterfield. Shauna had just turned ten and Robbie was seven, both of them too young to comprehend what had happened, but old enough to have to sit through it anyway. Hard to imagine Kenny as an uncle.

Adrian fits in here, with his paunch, looking more like a college teacher now, which he is. Kenny and I used to razz him years ago, when he was in university. He was the only one of all the guys we knew who went. I barely finished high school and Kenny dropped out halfway through grade ten. Adrian started wearing his hair in a pony tail, bought Earth shoes and told us to read Karl Marx. He was into this macrobiotic stuff too, so we'd order our steaks double thick and extra blue rare and talk about rifles and hunting. Kenny threatened to give him a haircut with a pair of tinsnips, the old construction worker's joke. But Adrian was always a sport and went along with us when we must have seemed pretty dumb.

He has this store he goes to now, he took me once. At the corner of Bloor and Yonge right downtown, Eddie Somebody, as if we're supposed to know. For people who get dressed up when they go camping. *His* store he called it. Very expensive, nothing like Ribtor's Surplus with the cases of Buck knives and bear repellant. With his button-down shirts and penny loafers, he looks like he shouldn't fit in, but he does somehow.

Kenny always idolized him, which irritated the hell out of me. Because he'd left, he'd made it in Kenny's eyes. Like an admission we were all losers if we stayed. Well I left too, but then again, I came back.

Adrian and Kenny were alike that way. Both of them always trying to be something else. Adrian with his hippie get-up and now his college look. With Kenny for a while it was Beatlemania. His hair cut, paisley shirt, black pointy-toed vinyl boots, and skin-tight salt and pepper jeans. Then it was the shag like Mick Jagger's. Kenny thought Toronto was like New York or Liverpool. A good place to be from. Deb and I used to spend weekends with Adrian and Lucia in Toronto. I didn't think it was so hot. They had their cowboys too. They just dressed in different clothes and talked faster and seemed sneakier, sort of, like they'd talk behind your back.

From the funeral home I recognized Lyle Weismore standing in the kitchen. Kenny used to drive for his small gravel outfit on and off, mostly off, but it was his first job. I nodded to him.

"Hey Tom. Ready for a real job yet, on the business end of a shovel?" One thing about Lyle, he always had a joke. Even if it wasn't funny.

"And just what end might that be, Lyle?" He was okay. He was just envious I had a government job. Lucky me.

Robert poured me a rye. Lyle's dressed low-key cowboy in pale blue permanent press Lee Riders. Unlike his old pal Larry Ridler, who's drinking coffee these days, but in an expensive Stetson, looking like a red-faced Glen Campbell with his new rawhide vest and silver heel and toe caps on his $300 Boulet boots. Eight hundred dollars worth of cowboy, and he's afraid of horses. But Lyle's old drinking buddy joined A.A., I'd heard. We pretended not to see each other. Lyle was okay because he knew when to stop. But Larry Ridler. They both used to race up and down 26th in Lyle's Fairlane, their hair greased back into ducktails, with Larry hanging out the window yahooing at the junior high girls sneaking smokes behind the I.G.A. Now he's Mr. Rhinestone Cowboy. But when Adrian came over, Larry livened up.

"Hi Tom. Hey, Professor." He shook my hand and then Adrian's, somewhat more enthusiastically. Adrian's not a real professor, he told me once himself.

"How long you out for?" Lyle asked him.

"A week. We're going to do some fishing," Adrian said, looking at me.

"Still going up to the lake? Brown trout good up there, I hear," Larry said, tipping his hat back the way movie cowboys do.

Brown trout were all fished out years ago and Larry Ridler didn't know the difference between a dry fly and a salmon egg. I wasn't having any part of this.

"Yeah, we're driving up early tomorrow," Adrian said.

I still remember Larry pounding out Kenny for wearing his hair long like Paul McCartney and then calling him a fairy. Now he's got the same haircut himself, fifteen years out of date, the phoney bugger.

I went to the front room to be with Ivy Dawes and the kids, and sat on the chair and ruffled the cat's back. Even that didn't help when I remembered helping Kenny scrub down his cat Fluffer when she rolled in the road after it was oiled. How she'd vomited for days and slowly we brought her back. Maybe I was wrong about coming — going somewhere else would be better right now. Like fishing.

Next morning, I got up with Deb. We have an understanding. She likes Adrian, but the old neighbourhood and guys like Kenny are bad news. That was then, she says, this is now. After she left for work, I started packing while Adrian took the truck and went to get Kenny. When he got back, I put the fishing rods into the rifle racks in the cab. After Deb's dad died I sold my guns, but kept the rifle racks as partial membership in the international brotherhood of arseholes and good ole boys. I loaded the food and the rest of our gear in the truck box. Adrian had good taste. His creel was wicker with genuine leather trim and brass fittings. It sure wasn't K-Mart.

After the truck was packed and the canoe loaded, I came back in and poured a coffee while Adrian changed. He'd left the urn, a sort of plastic jar really, made of the same material as a VCR case, on the mantelpiece. I was surprised how light it was, about the weight of a full can of beer or few handfuls of sand.

Kenny. So this is what it all came to. When I heard the hairdryer shut off, I went back to the kitchen and filled the thermos, spiking the coffee with a good shot of rye.

When Adrian came out to the truck, he had his shaving bag in one hand and Kenny in the other. He went to put them under the tarp in the back.

"Put him up front," I said, taking the shaving bag. "There's a vest under the seat."

Adrian looked over his glasses in a school-teachery way.

"Humour me," I said, and put the shaving bag under the tarp.

When I got in, Kenny was wrapped in my old down vest and wedged on top of the transmission hump between the firewall and the gear shift.

As we left the city on No. 2 North, the morning rush was easing, and as we cleared the city limits, I pushed the truck up to 130 K, ten safe ones over the limit. The lake where Gran parked her R.V. was two hours northwest of the city in the forestry reserve on the eastern slopes of the Rockies, just outside the Banff park boundary.

My eyes always relaxed and spread out a bit where the highway left the city and started its slow climb across the foothills. Highway 2 passes like a black plough mark through wide open fields of rippling yellow canola and wheat. Adrian seemed preoccupied, but I didn't dwell on it. With a bit of spiked coffee, some serious highway mileage, and some country tunes we'd both be fine, I figured. Nothing like country music to make you feel better. Patsy Cline, Maybelle Carter, Bob Wills and his Texas Playboys.

Our music, my mother used to say. Like the blues, feeling bad made you feel good. And what else can you do when you grow up in the home of one of the oldest country music radio stations in North America and the Calgary Exhibition and Stampede?

The voice of the announcer was nasal and perky when I turned on the radio.

"Coming up to the hour on CWBY — Voice of the Cowboy — in country music country. Welcome to all you visitors out there, and for all of you at home or on the road, here's two in a row to put you in the mood from our own Wilf Carter, and from the great big wonderful U.S. of A., Hank Williams, Senior."

Deb can't stand me playing country. She likes David Bowie. Kenny never listened to anything but the Beatles and the Stones. Adrian on the other hand is the only guy I know besides me who knows the words to "Ruby Don't Take Your Love To Town". And he still plays a fair banjo. One year we started a band and practised in his dad's garage. We only played a couple of gigs, once at the fall fair and at the community hall. Kenny was supposed to be our manager. People liked us, but then bluegrass and country went out of style.

" 'Blue Canadian Rockies', I haven't heard that one in years," Adrian said. "Ever heard the number he does on 'Old Shep'?"

"Yeah, there's a harp in the glove box," I said, relieved that Adrian seemed to be more talkative, "if you want to play along. Should be a C or G in there."

Driving was kind of healing too. I liked my job for that. Up at four, on the road by five. In the winter, I'd plough out the concession roads on my route. Breakfast by eight, off by two if there's no more snow and no call back. Cold and clear and alone, the way I like it. Turn the two-way down, so I can barely hear the dispatch, put the radio on the country station. In the summer we'd put the sidecutters on the tractors and cut the medians and sidehills, sometimes putting up signs or shovelling roadkill. On a good day, like the army ad says, there's no life like it.

Adrian says he envies me. A guy who makes sixty-five grand and has summers off. Maybe. Though I wouldn't want to be in Toronto again. Too many people.

We passed the thermos back and forth. I'd always liked Wilf Carter's yodel, but I never understood how yodelling became part of country music. Maybe the Swiss had something to do with it. Mountain music or something. We turned west off No. 2 onto 68, heading for 983. Out here the smaller the number, the bigger the road. When I'm not in a hurry I pick the road with the largest number.

"Mind if I turn it up? Wilf Carter's okay, but *this* is good." Adrian sang along in a good clear baritone with nasal in all the right places. I hummed harmony as the old and familiar voice crooned mournful and twangy as a dobro.

"Hank Williams," I said. "Senior."

"If country ever had a Shakespeare," Adrian nodded to me. "And you know something, we were all born the year Hank Williams died."

"Yeah and this one's called, 'I'll Never Get Out of This World Alive'."

"Isn't that the true thing?" Adrian turned quiet again and I wished I hadn't said anything. Even the coffee with its rye kicking in didn't seem to help him after that. He just tapped the harmonica end over end on the heel of his hand like a man worrying something. I didn't want to, but I just let it go.

983 begins about a half hour outside of Sundre where the road crosses the Red Deer River at the Mountain Aire Lodge. I figured we'd stop there and eat the sandwiches I'd

made and get some bait for the fish. After Sundre the road's gravel, but good gravel. And you know you're in bush country when farming is done with a D8 Cat pushing stumps rather than a John Deere pulling a disc.

Nobody had passed us in miles and now all the trucks coming the other way were highloaded with logs, their backdraft slapping the truck and tugging the wheel in my grip. Ahead of us were the mountains. Gran calls it God's country. With all those TV real estate salesmen hustling it for Him, I don't know if I'd go that far, but it sure as hell is good country. No white hats or fancy shirts here. Adrian finally seemed to be relaxing, sinking lower in his seat, his hand on the outside mirror, and while we still had another half hour's climb up into the lake, the city and everything in it seemed a dozen years in the future or the past, I wasn't sure. But he still wasn't talking about whatever was bothering him.

Just before we got to the lodge, we stopped to watch a small herd of horses driven by a couple of real cowboys, with yellow slickers tied to their saddles, going up to the alpine meadows above us. It was something you didn't see much anymore even out here, and the smell of pine on the dry breeze and even the dust kicking up under the truck smelled good in the mountain air. This was the West none of us dealt with well. I left it. Now I drive it. Deb keeps taking pictures, lining them all up on the table until she's got ten in a row showing the whole horizon. Then she realizes she didn't get the sky in. Kenny tried to ignore it. And Adrian too, until he comes home every other summer. But I was getting mad. I knew he didn't see this sort of sight at the corner of Bloor and Yonge or whatever it was. Finally I said what I'd wanted to for the last fifty miles.

"Something on your mind?"

He didn't respond right away, but he sat up and looked at me for the first time since we left Calgary.

"We'll talk about it."

"Okay." I can't stand not knowing. Even if I have an idea it's something I don't want to know. Like right now. Adrian had been anxious to talk to Lori and he had seemed even more upset after he came back with Kenny. I'd just thought maybe it was a mistake going back to get him after all.

"When we stop." He looked out the window. I'd have to wait.

The Mountain Aire Lodge was a collection of log buildings: a coffee shop and store, a gas bar in front, a barn with a corral out back and a few picnic tables alongside the bridge. The Red Deer River marked the eastern boundary of the forestry land we were travelling west into. Several pickups and a Highways grader were parked out front. Lunchtime.

There's an old story that if there's lots of trucks in front of a diner then it must be good. More likely it's either the only one around or the only one with a parking lot big enough for a rig. You learn this sort of thing in Highways. Everybody up here is either government, forestry or Highways, or oil or ranching. The rest are tourists. Like us.

We got our sandwiches and went out to the picnic tables beside the river. I ate mine quickly and finished the last of our coffee. Adrian didn't touch his. As we sat there, the wasps floated lazily in and out of the bushes along the river. The men inside the diner came out and the Highways grader stopped its idle ticking and popped diesel into the air as the stack opened up. This was ridiculous.

"Adrian, you going to tell me what's on your mind or what?" He picked up his sandwich and then dropped it.

"It wasn't alcohol, Tom. It was pneumonia."

By the way he looked at me, I knew this was something I should understand. He waited. I felt like the slow kid in his class.

"AIDS, Tom. He had AIDS. The doctor's report said he was so far gone that when he robbed that store he didn't care where he was."

Adrian got up and went back to the truck and sat there looking through the windshield. I didn't need to know this right now, or maybe ever. I had Kenny all figured out. Kenny the bullshit artist. King of the Road. But Kenny the swish? I had the stupid feeling that somehow I should have known. Kenny got Rhonda Robinson pregnant when they were both seventeen. She'd had an abortion. But we all knew she wanted to keep the kid. She never saw Kenny after that. It didn't add up, but maybe it did. Kenny had lied, and we'd all lied right along with him.

He used to hang out at a lot of bars and I saw him one night come out of the Continental, which was pretty high class for a guy who drove truck. He had his arm over some guy's shoulder. I'd pushed it to the back of my mind then. People did those kinds of things when they got drunk. And Kenny could talk, god he could talk. When he was on, both men and women liked him.

Another group of men came out and climbed into a forestry crew cab, slamming the doors, which jolted me. I threw the thermos under the tarp and got in beside Adrian. I was numb. My hands were stiff on the wheel. I looked at the jar wrapped in my old down vest. There wasn't just one Kenny Dawes, there were many.

In silence we drove up to the lake and set up camp, building a fire in the pit and airing out the R.V. Gran left parked there all summer. That night for supper I cooked big thick T-bone steaks over the coals of the woodfire, but neither of us really had any appetite, so most of it ended up in the firepit. I didn't like the idea of being bear bait. We drank a lot that night, which was stupid because neither of us are drinkers. The rum was Gran's. I hated rum and Adrian's old man was an alcoholic so he had his own reasons for not drinking. But we did anyway.

I couldn't get it out of my head.

"You sure it wasn't some prison thing he got?" I asked. Kenny was no muscle man and we'd all heard stories of guys in the can. It wasn't needles. Or was it? If Kenny had one redeeming quality, he wasn't a speed freak, so far as I knew.

"He'd had it for years. Lori also told me she'd caught him with an older guy once when they took a trip down to the States. He was fifteen at the time and he made her swear not to say anything." Across from me, the flames lit up Adrian's chin and mouth, but his eyes and forehead were shadows, as both of us stared into the white heat of the burning logs.

"He could've told us," I said. "At least you."

"Maybe in his own way he did, Tom. Besides, would it have made any difference?"

The wind swept up through the trees, and branches switched over our heads. With each gust, sparks from the firepit trailed up into the air. The sun had dropped over the mountains.

I looked at him. The guys we knew weren't exactly what you'd call understanding. Kenny was beaten down enough anyway. I wanted to believe it didn't matter to us either, but it did and we both knew it. It was one thing to read about it in the paper. It was also a lot easier to pretend to be something else than what you were.

"You remember the night those guys chased us in the park?" he asked.

A bunch of us had gone to a movie one Friday night after school. When the movie ended we got tired of waiting for the bus back uptown so we decided to walk. There was a shortcut through Central Park downtown we sometimes used during the day. By night it was supposed to be the fag park. But that night, we were walking alongside the park when a car load of greaseballs in black leather jackets went by. They slowed down beside us and yelled, "Faggots!" Then they pulled around the corner in front of us and waited with the lights off. We scattered, running with them chasing us. They didn't catch us, but I remember the long deliberate rasp of their heel clickers on the sidewalk, like a knife across a stone, as I lay hidden behind a hedge as they paced up the other side. I lay there listening to the thump of the Hollywood muffler until they left, my heart pounding in the grass. Even now when I hear one of those mufflers, my heart skips a beat.

"Remember how scared we were?" Adrian said, looking at me. "And we're straight."

We talked late that night and I put the kettle on and we diluted rum in hot water and added brown sugar and margarine to make an awful kind of toddy. Funny what tastes good around a fire.

Adrian was making up for lost time. Now he wanted to talk. I had to admit, in some ways, he knew Kenny better than I did. I'd avoided him the last few years. But

Adrian had the advantage of distance. Kenny reminded me too much of our old neighbourhood. Some people just never got away.

"Last time he phoned me Tom, was last fall. From his sister's. He always forgot about the time difference. Lucia hated it, so I'd take the phone in the other room. Some nights it was like he telephoned right into my dreams. Every two or three years he'd phone like that.

"Kenny remembered everything. Like he was still right there. Like my rabbits. When they got loose in the school on pet day and he went home and got his fishing rod and a carrot and lured them out of the crawl space. They were *my* rabbits and I'd forgotten that."

For a moment I was jealous. Maybe I'd never given him half a chance.

"He made me keep one of the litter for him. A runt he named. 'Remember Chopper,' he'd tell me. 'I'll never forget', he'd say. And he'd go on about how he was walking home that night down the back alley and he found this dead rabbit lying there. And he had to call me and tell me. Before he hung up, he said, 'You and me, we're not outsiders. I love you buddy.' "

Adrian wiped his nose with his new bandanna. Those fancy ones cost ten bucks. I'd learned a long time ago that if I held my eyeballs real tight and straight ahead the tears wouldn't leak out.

"Only two men ever told me that. Kenny and my father. Both of them were drunk. When I woke up the next morning I had to ask Lucia if he'd really called."

We said nothing more, but sat there for a long time before we bunked down in the R.V. There was only one bed, which we shared. All night I was conscious of Adrian beside me and every time his elbow touched my back, I flinched.

The next day we spent fishing. All we caught were a couple of small perch which we threw back. After lunch when Adrian motioned towards the truck where we'd left Kenny, I shook my head.

"Not yet," I said.

After supper that night, we put the dishes to boil in a basin on the grill and went down to the shore to drink our coffee. There was nothing more to say.

I looked at Adrian, and then out across the lake.

"I think it's time."

After I untied the canoe, Adrian shoved off through the cat-tails, with Kenny between us. I took the stern and steered us towards the far shore. The lake had been calm but as the sun set behind the mountains, the night wind coming down from their slopes pushed waves across the bow. The huge spruce and Douglas fir around the lake hushed and cracked. In an hour it would be dark.

A long, long time ago, we'd been out on the sidewalk with a hammer and a nail. Our bare knees scraped on the rough concrete as we squinted in concentration with the careful weight of the hammer held by its head so as not to buckle the lid of the pickle jar. Later, on the hill, fascinated with our jars full of bees, their fur bodies upside down scrambling against the holes for air, it was Kenny who was most afraid. Who loosened the lid of his jar and threw his furthest into the rolls of the grass and ran with the dark cloud of bees he was sure must be following him. The rest of us tipped ours with our toes and stood watching as they swarmed back towards the river, Kenny running the opposite way. Maybe that's all he ever did. Maybe that was his crime.

As we reached the middle of the lake, Adrian laid his paddle across the bow and I pulled back on mine to hold us steady into the rising wind, neither of us saying a word. What needed to be said would be spoken, if at all, in the years we had left. He turned and took the urn from inside the vest and lowered it, pouring it alongside the canoe. The dust from the ashes floated and spread on the waves. Then he placed the urn on the surface of the water where it too floated for a moment until a wave filled it and it sank out of sight. I looked at him as he stared out over the lake, his hands braced on the gunwales, knowing that the distance between us, me and this man I thought I knew, was as great as the distance now between us and Kenny. For a moment we rode over the rising waves. As the wind began to turn us, slowly I paddled back to the near shore and the low burning fire waiting for us there.

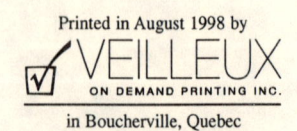

Printed in August 1998 by
VEILLEUX
ON DEMAND PRINTING INC.
in Boucherville, Quebec